CW01214264

# The Classic Bike Workshop

*by the same author*

| | |
|---|---|
| The Old Mechanic | Burringbah Books |
| stories of an old motorcycle mechanic | 2013 |
| | |
| Dominator in the Shadows | Amazon |
| more stories of an old motorcycle mechanic | 2020 |

# The Classic Bike Workshop

even more stories of an
old motorcycle mechanic

*Beautiful Jade Press*

Copyright Peter J. Uren 2014

Published in Australia
by Beautiful Jade Press
Raymond Terrace, NSW 2324

National Library of Australia Cataloguing-in-Publication entry
Author:            Uren, Peter, author.
Title:             The Classic Bike Workshop / Peter Uren.
ISBN:              9798-69315709-5 (paperback)
Dewey Number:      A823.4

First Amazon edition October 2020

*This book is copyright. Apart from any fair dealing for the purpose of private study, research, criticism or review as permitted under the Copyright Act, no portion of the material contained in this publication may be reproduced by any process without the written permission of the author.*

*This book is a work of fiction. All characters and events are fictional and any resemblance to real people and events is purely accidental, unless otherwise indicated.*

Cover design by the Author and KDP.
Back cover photograph courtesy of J.T. Macdonald, Bishop Norton, UK. Used with permission.

# Contents

| Chapter | Title | Page |
|---|---|---|
| 1 | Nothin' for Nothin' | 1 |
| 2 | Emeritus Mechanic | 9 |
| 3 | When Opportunity Knocks | 16 |
| 4 | Dollars and Sense | 23 |
| 5 | The Next Chapter | 31 |
| 6 | The Life of Riley | 38 |
| 7 | Walking the Walk | 46 |
| 8 | In the Club | 53 |
| 9 | Keeping Your Mind on the Job | 61 |
| 10 | When Only the Best Will Do | 69 |
| 11 | The Morning After | 78 |
| 12 | Variations on a Theme | 86 |
| 13 | Riding With Mates | 94 |
| 14 | An Obligation Fulfilled | 103 |
| 15 | Trading Classics | 111 |
| 16 | Bonnie, Sweet Bonnie | 119 |
| 17 | Beggars Can't Be Choosers | 127 |
| 18 | Testing Times | 135 |
| 19 | No Substitute for Cubes | 143 |
| 20 | Keeping Up With Kieran | 151 |
| 21 | I've Been Everywhere Man | 158 |
| 22 | A Deadly Spike | 166 |
| 23 | Impossible Choices | 173 |
| 24 | An Unexpected Delivery | 181 |
| 25 | The Important Things in Life | 189 |

# Dedication

Many of those who ride motorcycles live to ride – riding motorcycles is their passion. As I wrote in my last book, their view is that "any day is a good day when you can ride". But sadly, too many of those who love riding, do not return home. I have had my fair share of motorcycle accidents and I have the scars to prove it. But I was fortunate – I lived to ride again. If your passion is riding, remember: ride to live. This book is dedicated to those who did not survive the ride.

# Acknowledgements

A book is only as good as its writer, and a writer is only as good as the people who support him, or her. I am indebted to several groups of people.

Without good editors, there would be a multitude of errors, from simple spelling mistakes to poor grammar. So, I would like to extend my heartfelt thanks to Stewart Upton and Elizabeth Bradhurst, without whom my story would be full of errors.

I was able to acquire the services of my new technical expert: Steve Lewis. Steve is the owner of the very delectable Norton ES2 Special on the front cover. Without the efforts of Steve, the "rivet counters" would have a field-day – thanks.

I would also like to thank Chris Pickett and his team – Dennis Penzo and Bec Eastment – at the Australian motorcycle magazine, *Cycle Torque*. Not only has Chris provided the Foreword for this book, he has supported me by having my books reviewed in, and by offering them for sale through, the magazine.

Finally, how could I ever forget the folk at Stroud Writers? They have been supporting me since I first put pen to paper; and not just this book, but both of my previous books, as well as my short stories and poems. Their ongoing critiquing of each chapter of this story has been invaluable.

# Foreword

Peter Uren's first book, *The Old Mechanic*, told the tale of an old bloke, working away in an old ramshackle shed behind his house. It could be any old shed in any Australian town. He catered for old blokes much like himself, blokes who shared a passion with the old mechanic for old bikes. I enjoyed reading that first story very much; it is written in an easy to read style, and Peter, the author, gave the reader a detailed insight into the culture that exists around the classic motorcycle scene. I particularly enjoyed the way he interacted with the young local 'modern' bike rider, and how when the young rider became his apprentice, the workshop dynamic changed. It was also a story of family and some of life's troubles, the ones that get thrown up every now and then.

Then came *Dominator in the Shadows*. It is a continuation of the same theme, but delves further into the relationships surrounding the workshop and the family. It also sees some of the characters chasing their dreams, dreams that have been put on the back burner for many years. I especially loved this part of the story because dreams are such a huge part of classic motorcycle ownership.

This latest instalment of the trilogy is expected to take things even further. I am looking forward to reading it, and if it is anything like the two previous instalments, I think you will love reading it too.

**Chris Pickett**
Editor
Cycle Torque Magazine
www.cycletorque.com.au

# Preface

When I first started writing fiction in mid-2012, I started writing about the passion of my life: motorcycles. I did not set out to write a book – that happened almost by accident – I actually started writing a short story. Indeed, that is why the first chapter of *The Old Mechanic* is only about 1,350 words. It was never supposed to be a full-size book; I just continued writing in response to feedback from friends who read it. I did not even have a plot sorted out until I had written the first seven or eight chapters. When I realised that I needed to plan the rest of the story, I merely wrote down the chapter headings in place of a plot.

The different characters in my three books are not real people. However, most of them are an amalgam of people whom I have met or had dealings with over the years. But anyone who knows me well would see aspects of me in Michael, and the relationship he has with the old mechanic is the one I would love to have had with my father, but never did. Now, while the storyline and all the characters are fictional, all of the anecdotes of the old mechanic are true; all of them really happened.

My second book, *Dominator in the Shadows*, was written following the positive feedback I received from my first book. That *The Old Mechanic* was so well received came as a real surprise to me, so much in fact that I doubted whether I should publish it at all. Still, I was determined that my second novel would be even better. But rather than writing more of the same, and again following feedback received from a few of my readers, I realised that I needed to develop the characters more. So, the second book was more about the people, rather than the processes. I also needed to tidy up some loose ends that were left hanging at the end of my first book. Nevertheless, it followed the same successful formula set by my first novel; that of restoring a classic British motorcycle.

I started writing my third book, *The Classic Bike Workshop*, even before I had launched *Dominator in the Shadows*. But the gestation period this time was long and tortuous. I did not want this one to be so similar to the previous two that my readers would become bored. Yet I did not want to alienate those same readers by writing something that was too different. This time around, the old mechanic has handed the reins of the workshop to his one-time apprentice, Michael. But while he is no longer in charge, the old mechanic is still in the picture. Kieran also plays a much more prominent role in the story. And just like in my second novel, I have spent more time developing the characters. Indeed, the characters play a more prominent role in the story than the motorcycles.

After writing *Dominator in the Shadows* and before I started *The Classic Bike Workshop*, I attended a writer's workshop. The lady who ran the workshop taught me a very important lesson which was that the simplest and easiest way to get from Point A to Point B is a straight line. But writing about a straight line can be terribly boring. What makes the journey interesting is the obstacles placed in the way between the two points. The story is then how the various characters deal with those obstacles. Having learned the lesson, I was determined to put it into action. But I will leave it to you, my reader, to assess whether I have been successful or otherwise.

In this story, I deal with a number of difficult subjects, not least being the death of one of the main characters in a motorcycle accident. As the creator of the character, even though he was merely a figment of my imagination, I had to deal with some very real emotions, like grief, when he died. It took me more than a fortnight to deal with the issues raised. But there will be some readers who have had to deal with the death of real people as the outcome of a motorcycle accident. I could not hope to plumb the depths of sadness that some of you will have experienced as a result. But the point is, riding a motorcycle comes with a level of risk to life and limb that is not shared with many other forms of transport. It does not matter how good a rider you are, or how long you have been riding, motorcycle riding is a dangerous activity.

There are those who *live to ride*. They eat, drink and breathe motorcycles. Riding is their number one passion, their *raison d'être*. I used to be like that. I used to love going to work because it was another opportunity to ride, and I used to love going home for the same reason. I rode my motorcycle on weekends with my friends, and at every opportunity I had. Then I had a serious accident that almost took my leg and left me hospitalised for about three months. At that time, my family had to deal with their own very real emotions when they saw me laid up in the hospital. My accident was also a wake-up call for me. It made me realise that it is all well and good for you to *live to ride*, but how important it was for you to also *ride to live*.

**Peter J. Uren**

# Chapter 1

## NOTHIN' FOR NOTHIN'

Celebrating a 60$^{th}$ birthday is a momentous occasion in the life of most people; that was certainly the case for Jim Browning. Not only did it mark the end of another decade of survival as a motorcyclist on NSW roads, but the week following his birthday, he was made redundant from his position as Workshop Foreman at Redscape Manufacturing in Tamworth. That was also the time that his wife informed him that she was leaving after 36 years of marriage.

Any one of these events would be enough for most men to cope with. Jim, however, took each in his stride. It certainly helped that the separation from his wife was amicable; indeed, he felt somewhat relieved. As so often happens with married couples, unless they have a common interest and continue to work on their relationship, they drift apart until they reach a point when they see no reason to remain together.

Once their children had left home to pursue careers of their own – a son in the military and a daughter in interior design – his wife decided she wanted to "find herself". The last Jim heard, she had moved to the North Coast of NSW, and was living on a hippy commune outside of Nimbin. That Jim was tired of working also helped, and so he probably would have jumped if he had not been pushed. His redundancy payment helped seal the deal.

Jim had been riding motorcycles since, well, for as long as he could remember. His earliest memory was of an old pre-war rigid-framed AJS 350 that he and his older brother Ron used as a "paddock basher" on his uncle's farm in the early 1960s. While most kids learned to ride on a bicycle, he learned on the Ajay. His father had had a variety of bikes as the boys were growing up: BSAs and Triumphs mainly, always in various states of disrepair. To the young Jim, his father seemed to be forever working on his motorcycle, instead of riding it. Something on the bike constantly needed his attention: whether an adjustment, lubrication, an oil change or a repair that needed carrying out and, no matter what he did, there was always a puddle of oil beneath the engine.

So, when Jim completed his trade course and had saved enough money, he was determined to purchase a motorcycle he could ride, day in, day out, and one that he would not have to spend all his spare time fixing. The first new bike he purchased was a Honda CB750 in 1972. He absolutely loved the machine and rode it to work every day, and with his mates every weekend. A succession of UJMs followed over the years, as his finances improved and his domestic circumstances settled down. It even got to the point that if his bike needed repair or a service, he could afford to pay a mechanic to do the work. But while the Japanese manufactured bikes were as reliable as the proverbial Swiss watch, Jim soon came to the realisation that they lacked a certain intangible attribute that bikes made in Britain, Europe and America had in spades: character.

So, when Triumph started making motorcycles again in the 1990s, Jim's interest was aroused. His initial impression was that they were just like Japanese machines with a British name. But as the number and variety of new models arrived in Australia to widespread acclaim by the local media, he began to take more notice. Jim's first Triumph was a 955cc Sprint triple. He enjoyed riding it and did so whenever he had the opportunity. After 12 years' ownership, and now with a back that was failing from wear and tear and arthritis, he decided to get a motorbike with a more upright riding position: what is known in the trade as a "standard". With limited choices due to his short stature, he went for a "retro" model that harked back to his formative years – a new Triumph Bonneville T100 SE.

Jim loved his new acquisition, although he quickly realised that, while the bike shared its name with the sporty Triumph Bonnevilles of the 1960s and 70s, in his view the motorcycle was more a case of style winning out over substance. Sure they were very reliable and the seat was extremely comfortable, but his bike lacked power and the suspension was very basic. Trolling through the internet one evening, he eventually found what he was looking for: advice on modifications to the front forks and the rear shock absorbers, and suggestions to enable a modest performance boost without impacting reliability.

After divvying up his redundancy payout, the proceeds from the sale of their home and both superannuation savings accounts, Jim was left with enough money to purchase a small unit for himself to live in, and an annuity so that he would be comfortable for the rest of his life, unless of course if he lived to 105! He even had enough for the occasional holiday and, most important of all, to continue to indulge his passion for riding.

The unit Jim purchased was at the rear in a complex of three on a quiet street in Banjo Creek. The Estate Agent informed him that, as far as he knew, the other two units were owner occupied, which suited Jim – in his experience, owners were quieter than renters and they were generally better at looking after their properties.

With his time now his own, he could move in at his leisure. While the unit was still relatively new and in good condition, the décor was not to his liking. He took the opportunity, while it was empty, to repaint the walls from a girly pink to a more neutral pale blue for the bathroom and beige for the other rooms, and to replace the light off-white carpets with a hard-wearing floating timber floor that would not show the dirt as much, and would be easier to clean and maintain.

Because his wife now eschewed all material possessions, Jim was able to buy out her share of their furniture and household goods, which had the added benefit that he would not have to purchase new furnishings for the unit. He stored most of what he owned in his garage while he repainted the walls and changed the flooring. He had moved into a cabin in the local caravan park, and he relied on his motorcycle as his sole form of transport, other than walking. The local hardware store offered free delivery which he gratefully accepted.

It was not until after he had started redecorating that he got to meet some of his neighbours. Early one Saturday morning on his return from the local supermarket with his hands full of grocery bags, Jim spied a young couple driving a Volkswagen Golf out of the driveway. Unable to wave, he nodded to them while they gesticulated wildly in return. Later in the day he answered a knock to his front door. He opened it to the same young couple.

'Hello, welcome to the neighbourhood,' replied the young woman. 'I'm Katie …'

'… And I'm Michael.'

'G'day, I'm Jim. For a horrible moment there I thought you were going to say you were Jehovah's Witnesses,' he replied with a smile.

Michael and Katie laughed.

'I'd invite you in for a cuppa, but as you can see I'm redecorating.'

'That's alright,' replied Katie, 'we only wanted to say hello and welcome. When do you move in properly?'

'As soon as I've finished painting, and the carpets are replaced. All my furniture's in the garage, so I'll be moving in then.'

'If I'm not working, I'll give you a hand to move if you like,' said Michael.

'Sure. Where do you work?'

'I'm a motorcycle mechanic. I work at Classic Bike Repairs and Service over on the highway south of Tamworth.'

'Really? I ride a motorbike.'

'Yeah? Is that your Triumph Bonneville?'

'Yeah, I've had it for about six months now. Do you ride?'

'Of course. I've got an old Norton 500 single. I ride it to work when Katie's got the car.'

'Do ya moonlight?'

'What do you mean?'

'You know, do ya do work away from the workshop?'

'No, not really; my weekends are usually pretty full doing domestics. Why, do you need some work done on your Trumpy?'

'Yeah, just some performance mods … but that's alright, I'll find someone.'

'Doesn't your Bonnie go hard enough?'

'My last bike was a Sprint triple, so the twin's lacking a few berries in comparison.'

'You'll never get it to go as hard as the Sprint.'

'Yeah, I know that, but I wouldn't mind if it could go just a little bit quicker and handle better.'

'What mods do you have in mind?'

'Just a few things to make it breathe a bit better: change the exhaust, remove the air box, change the air filters, and remove the air injection. Once that's done the ECU'll need remapping. And then I can work on the shockies.'

'Why don't you get the local Triumph dealer to do the mods if you can't do them yourself? They supply most of that stuff anyway, don't they?'

'Yeah, but they also charge like a wounded bull.'

'Well, you get nothin' for nothin'. I tell you what, you get the parts and I'll help you fit them. Then just get the dealer to do the remapping.'

'That'd be great, thanks. Well, I'd better be getting back to work.'

'And we've got housework to do,' added Katie who was starting to pull on Michael's shirt-tail, 'or you'll be getting nothin' for nothin'.'

'Ah, the things we do for love,' declared Michael as he followed close behind.

Jim turned his attention back to repainting the kitchen and living room. He had already completed the bathroom, toilet and laundry, with the two bedrooms still to do. The flooring contractor was due the following Thursday, so he had less than a week to finish his work. A professional painter would have been quicker, but he had better things to do with his money than to pay for a job he could do himself.

The young couple in the front unit, Katie and Michael, appeared to be quite friendly. The neighbours in the other unit next to his were a retired couple who kept pretty much to themselves, which suited Jim. Neighbours could sometimes be a bit hit and miss. He preferred the kind who were there for when they were needed, but who minded their own business at other times. But he was glad for one thing: he had found someone who could relate to his passion for riding.

And speaking of riding, he had not taken his Triumph out for a decent fang since his marriage break-up, and so he was hanging out. But that would have to wait until he had finished moving in. As he worked, he began to imagine how the Bonneville would perform with the engine and suspension modifications. He hoped they would not show up deficiencies in other areas like tyres and wheel rim sizes. That was the problem with changing one thing, he thought, there would always be something else that would need attention as a consequence.

Working all weekend and late into the evenings on Monday and Tuesday, Jim finished painting mid-afternoon on the Wednesday. He was packing up when he received a text message on his mobile. It was from the flooring contractor confirming that he would be there at 7:00 am the following morning. Looks like my sleep-in will have to wait until Saturday, thought Jim.

With aching shoulders, arms and back, he fell into bed that evening and slept soundly all night, only waking when his alarm sounded at 6:00 am. He arose, showered, shaved and dressed. He would have breakfast in his unit. There was a heavy fog outside and his bike was wet from dew. After wiping it down with a chamois, he started it to warm the motor while he donned his jacket, helmet and gloves.

The roads were damp and the visibility poor, so he was grateful that the traffic was light. He was riding down his street as Michael was going the other way, presumably to work. They waved briefly as they passed. Jim had just poured cereal into a bowl when the flooring contractor arrived.

'I'm just about to make a cuppa; do ya want one?'

'No thanks mate, I 'ad one before I left 'ome. Besides, the sooner I get the job done, the sooner you c'n move in.'

'Are you workin' alone?'

'Yeah, me offsider's taken crook.'
'Well, if ya need a hand, just say so.'
'You c'n 'elp me unload if ya like?'
'Can do.'

Jim did more than just unload. He performed the job of contractor's assistant. The contractor was so thankful that he dropped his quoted price by half the amount that he would have had to pay a labourer. Jim was doubly pleased because the entire job was finished soon after lunch on the Friday. With Michael's help, he moved in over the weekend.


UJM – Universal Japanese Motorcycle: a term coined in the mid-1970s by the American *Cycle* magazine to cover a particular type of Japanese standard motorcycle that became commonplace following the ground-breaking Honda CB750, considered to be the first "Superbike". With its inline four-cylinder engine, the CB750 became a template for subsequent designs from the other three Japanese manufacturers. Stereotypically, a "UJM" would be a 4-cylinder standard motorcycle with a carburettor for each cylinder, a unit construction engine, a disc front brake, a conventional tubular cradle frame, telescopic front forks and twin-shock rear suspension. (Wikipedia)

# Chapter 2

## EMERITUS MECHANIC

After more than 50 years working, servicing, repairing and restoring classic British motorcycles, like many men in similar circumstances, the old mechanic had difficulty adapting to retirement. Despite his best intentions of taking life easier after he had completed the Vincent restoration, and since he had found the bike of his dreams, the Norton Dominator 99 650SS, he quickly discovered that life away from the workshop was anything but exciting.

Initially, his attention had been taken up with his new bike. Unlike many modern sport motorcycles, there is little by way of easy adjustment to the suspension of their classic equivalents. Nevertheless, the quantity and viscosity of oil in the forks, and spring rates in both forks and shock absorbers, can be changed to suit the individual preferences of the rider, and the style of riding planned. Other things that can be changed to suit the rider are positioning of the handlebars, brake, clutch and gearshift levers.

Once he had the Norton to his liking, the old mechanic packed some gear into a pair of throwover saddlebags and, with a rucksack on his back, went for a long ride down the east coast highways to Melbourne and back via the Snowy Mountains, staying with relatives and friends along the way. The bike was everything he had ever imagined it would be. But he had returned home less than a week before boredom began to set in.

It was now mid-summer. Day-time temperatures were in the mid to high 30s on most days. Occasionally there was relief from the heat as storms would sweep in from the southwest over the sun-drenched plains pushing walls of dust ahead of the front. Sometimes there was a torrential downpour and even hail to accompany the storm, but more often than not there was just thunder, lightning and wind. Lightning strikes would invariably ignite the tinder-dry bushland creating raging bushfires. Summer in the New England was as hot as the winters were cold. At least the hot and dry climate was more conducive to riding a motorcycle. Still, there is only so much riding one person alone can do.

With a north-westerly wind blowing, bringing the searing heat from the NSW outback, the old mechanic tossed and turned during the night. While his little cottage was insulated against the winter cold, without the benefit of air conditioning, once his house had heated up there was precious little he could do to cool it down again other than open the windows. At 1:00 am he arose from his bed and took a cold shower. He did not bother to dry himself, but rather stood dripping wet under the ceiling fan. He was almost cold when he went back to bed.

He woke again just as the sun was peeping over the horizon. He thought about the day ahead, and what he would do. There were any number of jobs around the house that needed his attention, with painting being the most urgent. The house had not been painted since before his wife was diagnosed with cancer over eight years previously. But on a scale of 1 to 10 of his most favoured jobs, painting rated below zero, especially in the middle of a hot summer. The old mechanic was a great believer in horses for courses, and that people should only do what they were good at. As a house painter, he believed he made a good motorcycle mechanic. All the other small tasks, he convinced himself, could wait for the cooler months.

As he boiled the jug and toasted slices of bread for his breakfast, he began to wonder how busy the two younger mechanics had been over the summer months. He had studiously avoided visiting the workshop since getting his Norton on the road because of the assurances he had given to Michael that, in retirement, he would not have time to be bored. But he missed their company, and especially the times they would meet over a cuppa to discuss the day ahead. He loved the banter and watching the others learn as mechanics, and grow and mature as young men.

Most of all he missed Katie. In the period before she had moved out, he had become used to her cooking his meals and making the treats to be shared with the others in the workshop. But in particular he missed her companionship. Just having someone else in the house, even if they were sleeping or just watching television, meant he could forget about his loneliness. Since his return from his ride, living by himself seemed to accentuate his feelings of loss. He was determined to do something about it, but he was not sure what.

The sound of activity outside drew him to the kitchen window. He saw Michael and Kieran already accepting customer bikes for repair or maintenance and caught a glimpse of Katie in her office preparing orders and invoices. He suddenly realised that he was the only thing missing from the scene outside. He quickly finished his tea and toast, completed his ablutions and dressed in his overalls. He felt somewhat reinvigorated when he walked the 50 or so paces from his back door to the workshop.

'Morning Michael, morning Kieran, morning my sweetheart,' he called as he entered.

'Mornin' George,' replied Kieran.

Katie came running from the office and threw her arms around her father's neck and kissed him on the cheek. 'Morning dad,' she replied breathless with excitement.

Michael stood with his mouth agape, staring at his father-in-law.

'What's the matter Mike, cat gotcha tongue?'

'No, I just didn't expect to see you back in the workshop so soon dressed in your "overies".'

'Well, I just wanted to see if you needed a hand.'

'It wouldn't have anything to do with you being bored now, would it?'

'As the saying goes Mike, "Ask no questions and you'll be told no lies".'

The old mechanic made his way over to the sink where he located his old enamel mug in the cupboard. He filled the jug and flicked the switch. The surrounds were all familiar, even though Katie had added a feminine touch with clean tea-towels and new containers for the tea-bags and sugar in place of the old jars.

'I've really missed you three,' said the old mechanic as he waited for his tea to draw.

'Yeah, we haven't seen much of you since you got back from down south,' said Michael. 'How was the trip?'

'It was great, especially coming back through the Snowies. I reckon the engineers who planned those roads must've been bikers.'

'"Owd'ja Dommie go?' asked Kieran.

'Better than sex,' he replied in a stage whisper.

'How was that dad?' asked Katie.

'It was terrific sweetheart.'

'Ya know I've gotta new bike,' continued Kieran.

'No, I didn't know. Whad'ja buy?'

'A '63 Bonnie; the firs' of the unit construction T120s.'

'Oh nice! Whadya gonna do with your Yammie?'

'We 'aven't decided yet. Prob'ly keep it.'

'What condition's the Bonnie in?'

'Basket case, but we godit cheap on eBay. Dad's gonna 'elp me restore it.'

'Well I'm sure it'll keep both you and your dad off the streets for a while. Whad'ja mum have to say?'

Kieran smiled, 'She don't know yet.'

'So, how's your love life?'

As Kieran replied, he blushed. 'Awright I guess.'

Katie added, 'Kieran's getting baptised next Sunday.'

The old mechanic turned from Kieran to Katie and back to Kieran. 'Really?'

'Yeah, Kieran's got all religious,' proclaimed Michael with a look verging on contempt.

'I 'ave not,' he replied defensively.

'Don't you pay any attention to the mockers, Kieran. I take it you've been going to church with Lilly.'

'Yeah, you said to do whatever it takes …'

'Good for you. Can I come?'

'To the baptism?'

'Yeah.'

'Of course, if ya wanna.'

'I'd love to.' Then, turning to Michael, the old mechanic asked, 'So what's on the agenda for today Mike?'

'Are you sure you wanna do some work?'

'Well I didn't get dressed in these,' pointing to his overalls, 'to play tiddlywinks.'

Michael looked around the workshop at the array of customer motorcycles. Some were in for a general service: grease and oil change, some for brake pads, one for a new speedometer cable, and another for a new drive chain.

'The Beeza Super Rocket needs the wheel bearings replaced, so you can start on that if ya like?'

'Sounds, good. Do we have any spares?'

Katie responded first, 'Yeah, in the storeroom.'

When the old mechanic entered the storeroom, he noticed with satisfaction some important changes that had been made. Everything was now neatly arranged on the shelves, with the spares labelled and identified by make and model. On the wall, there were lists of spares held with instructions to cross them from the list as they were consumed. This was so, at any time, Katie could see what spares were being held in the inventory, and what needed to be ordered.

When he left the storeroom with the parts in hand, the old mechanic was met by Michael. 'Can we have a word?'

'Sure, what's on your mind?'

'Outside.'

The old mechanic was puzzled, but obediently followed Michael out into the laneway between the workshop and his small cottage. Once outside, the two men faced each other.

'I thought you'd left me in charge.' Michael's voice had a bitter edge to it.

'You are in charge.'

'But it can't work if there're two bosses.'

'There aren't two bosses Mike; you're the boss, you're in charge.'

'But what if the others come to you for advice 'n stuff?'

'Then I'd give it to them.'

'But you'd be undermining my authority.'

'Mike, there's a difference between giving people advice and guidance and having authority over them. You're right, there can't be two bosses. As far as the business is concerned, you're in charge. You set the priorities; you give the orders and directions; you pay the bills. But I've still got something to contribute Mike. I have a wealth of knowledge concerning classic British motorbikes, and I'm offering it to you free of charge. I tried retirement – it sucks.'

'You don't want to be paid?' asked Michael incredulously.

'Nope. Seeing the business thriving and you and Katie happy is payment enough. You've heard of an Emeritus Professor?'

'Yeah.'

'Think of me as an Emeritus Mechanic.'

# Chapter 3

## WHEN OPPORTUNITY KNOCKS

The old mechanic settled quickly into his working routine, happy in the knowledge that the business finances and the day-to-day decisions were now the responsibility of someone else. As he worked, he thought about how his relationship with Michael had changed since he had left and then returned. He had not anticipated that confrontation on his first day back on the job. The last thing he wanted was for there to be tension between himself and Michael, or to undermine his position of authority. He realised that he would need to be a little more circumspect in his dealings with the others in the workshop, as well as his dealings with their customers.

The three mechanics took a break for their mid-morning smoko. Katie joined the trio as they waited for the jug to boil. She broke the silence.

'It's good to have you back working with us Dad. I didn't think you would've lasted long as a retiree.'

'Why do you say that?' asked the old mechanic.

'You're just not the type to sit back with your feet up while the others around you are working.'

Michael, who had been relatively quiet since his confrontation with the old mechanic, finally spoke. 'Isn't that what I said? But I'm not sure there's gonna be enough work for all of us.'

All eyes turned toward Michael. Katie gave a look of dismay.

He paused before continuing. 'At least, not unless we make some changes.'

'Whad'ja 'ave in mind?' asked Kieran.

He paused again. 'I've been thinking: there's plenty of work for two mechanics, maybe for two and a half, but there's not really enough for three.'

'Are you saying you don't want me working here?' asked the old mechanic aggrieved.

'Absolutely not! What I'm saying is that you being here's giving us an opportunity to expand the business.'

'How so?'

'Well ... like it or not, your expertise is in classic motorcycle restorations. We've seen it both in a high-end bike like the Vincent Black Shadow, and in a bread 'n butter model like my Norton ES2.'

'There's not much money to be made in bikes like your Norton.'

'That's why we'd need to stick to the higher end of the market; bikes like Norton Dominators and Commandoes, Velocettes and Vincents. When we're really busy, you can give Kieran and me a hand, but when it's quiet, you can go back to whatever it is you're restoring. And when it's really quiet, we can give you a hand. What do ya think?'

The old mechanic thought about the idea for a few moments. 'I'm not sure there's a lot of money to be made in restoring classic bikes, and there's always the danger of over-capitalising.'

'Whad'ya mean?' asked Kieran.

'Spending more money on the bike and restoration than you can sell it for.'

'The biggest cost in any restoration is the labour component,' argued Michael. 'If you're offering to work for nix, labour costs will be negligible.'

'Yes, but you still need to factor it in, and then there'll still be outsourcing costs for things we can't do in-house: things like chrome-plating, powder-coating, spray painting and such,' added the old mechanic. 'Still, you never know until you try. Where're you gonna find a bike to restore?'

'So, do you think it's a goer?' asked Michael.

'I don't see why not. How long have you been thinking about this idea of yours?'

Michael glanced at his watch. 'Hmm, about an hour or so,' he said grinning.

The old mechanic frowned before repeating his question. 'Where're you gonna find a bike to restore?'

'The usual places: eBay, swap meets, the classifieds, word o' mouth.'

'Well, whatever you do, check with me first before you commit to buying anything.'

'Of course.'

After Katie had returned to her office and Michael went back to servicing a Matchless 500, Kieran asked the old mechanic, 'Is my Bonnie at the 'igh end of the market?'

'Triumph Bonnevilles are very popular Kieran, but there're also a lot of 'em around. When you're restoring one for yourself, like you are, it doesn't really matter how much you spend. But if you're doing it to make a profit, like we are, then there's more money to be made in the rarer, higher value bikes like a Velocette or a Vincent, and to a lesser extent in some Nortons.'

Kieran looked downcast, so the old mechanic continued. 'There're a lot of variables to consider: like how much you paid and the condition of the bike, what needs to be done, the availability of parts and what you could sell one for. But don't worry Kieran, you can lose just as much, and often a lot more, on a Vincent as you can on a Bonneville.'

The old mechanic resumed his responsibility of replacing the wheel bearings on the BSA Super Rocket. As he worked on the rear wheel, he thought about Michael's proposal. While there were aspects of the Vincent Black Shadow restoration that had been frustrating, especially dealing with the customer, waiting for him to make a decision, he realised with satisfaction that he would not have those frustrations because he would be making the crucial decisions himself, even if Katie and Michael would be the ones paying the bills. The customer was being taken right out of the decision-making process.

Just as long as the right bike was bought for the right price, he reasoned, there would be no downside to the plan. The more he thought about it, the more excited he became. And then it dawned on him that the business was in good hands; Michael may have been a fairly average motorcycle mechanic, but he had the makings of being a very successful businessman.

Katie had taken over the role of fetching the lunchtime sandwiches for the three mechanics, the rationale being that Kieran was more valuable to the workshop as a mechanic than he was as an errand boy. It also gave her the opportunity to influence changes to their collective diets by ordering wholegrain breads, salads and fruits. Her return signalled that it was time for lunch.

The old mechanic opened his sandwich, noticing that the bread was different. He looked around and saw that everyone else had the same wholegrain bread.

'What's with the crunchy bread? What happened to the good old white sandwich loaf?'

'I made the change,' declared Katie defiantly. 'One of the biggest causes of bowel cancer is a diet that's high in fats and sugars and low in dietary fibre. I figured that we could all do with the healthy option.'

The old mechanic looked at Kieran. 'Whadya reckon Kieran?'

'I don' mind the taste, an' if it's good for ya, that's a bonus.'

'Yeah, I s'pose it is.'

The old mechanic turned to Michael who was happily munching away on his sandwich. 'So, how're you going to finance this plan of yours? Are you gonna borrow from the bank?'

'That's a possibility, but I don't really want to go into debt just in case it doesn't work out. I'm actually thinking of selling my Norton.'

All eyes turned toward Michael in surprise.

'But I thought you loved that bike,' asserted the old mechanic.

'I do, but I'm not *in* love with it.'

'But you won't 'ave a bike to ride,' said Kieran.

'I get plenty of opportunities test-riding customer bikes.'

'But what about weekends?' asked the old mechanic.

'Our weekends are pretty full-on now without riding.'

'But what about when Katie needs the car to go to her other job?' countered the old mechanic.

Michael took a deep breath before answering. 'She can drop me off or I can get a lift from Kieran.' He scanned the circle of faces looking at him. 'It's not like I'm selling a family heirloom – it's just a motorbike.'

'Yes, but you put – we put – a lot of blood, sweat and tears into restoring it,' argued the old mechanic. He looked at Michael who seemed resolute in his decision. 'But you're right, it is only a motorbike. I just hope you don't regret it later on.'

'I think I'd regret more having an opportunity to expand the business and not acting on it. And besides, if Kieran's getting a Triumph Bonneville, I'll need something better so I can keep up.'

Everyone laughed, easing the tension.

Later that evening, after the old mechanic had finished his dinner and completed the washing up, he turned on his laptop computer and started searching for a suitable classic motorcycle to restore. As he expected, finding the right bike at a reasonable price was proving to be as great a challenge as he expected the actual restoration would be. But as the old saying goes, it costs nothing to look.

After about two hours trolling through several different classified advertising websites, he had located a total of five classic motorcycles that might make suitable candidates for restoration. While none was in "basket-case" condition, and further investigation would be necessary to ensure mechanical integrity, he considered that, with a mild cosmetic refresh, he could on-sell them turning a good profit in a relatively short space of time.

However, there was still the matter of getting the cash to bankroll the first purchase. As he logged off and shut the computer down, he thought again about the Norton ES2 that Michael said he would put up for sale. While he had been happy enough to sell it to Michael in the first place, that old Norton held a special place in his memory. Even though the Norton Dominator 99 650SS was the bike he had always coveted, the "Easy 2" was a good, honest, reliable machine, that anyone could afford and ride. He went to sleep thinking of alternatives to selling the old Norton. He was not the only one.

'How much do you think you'd get selling the Norton?' asked Katie the next morning.

Michael thought about the question before replying. 'I don't know really, maybe eight to ten thousand, maybe a bit more. I won't know until I put it on the market and see if I get any offers.'

'What would it take to keep it?'

Michael looked up from his breakfast cereal; Katie's face showed no emotion. 'Don't you want me to sell it?'

'We've had a lot of good times on that old bike: picnics, rides through the national park. And if you hadn't been out for a ride that day, you would never have become my "accidental hero", and we might never have become friends, let alone lovers.' Suddenly a tear started to course down her cheek.

Michael jumped to his feet, taking Katie in his arms. She buried her face into his shoulder and sobbed. 'I didn't realise that old Norton meant so much to you.'

In a muffled voice she replied, 'I didn't realise either … 'til last night.' She pulled away from him and grabbed a tissue from a box on the breakfast bar, and wiped her eyes and blew her nose.

'Do you want me to keep it?' asked Michael.

'Mikey, do whatever you think is best.'

# Chapter 4

## DOLLARS AND SENSE

As Michael made his way to the workshop, he thought about how he could raise the money to buy the motorcycle to restore without having to sell his Norton. Katie had taken him by surprise when she expressed such an emotional attachment to the old machine. While he parked his bike, he had to agree with her that they had had some good times riding it together.

Even though the business had been picking up over the warmer months, he knew from past experience that the work would slow to a trickle again during winter months. That was one more reason to instigate another means of increasing turnover. Even though the accumulation of wealth had never been a strong motivator for Michael, he did consider that it was always better to be richer than poorer.

The old mechanic had already opened the workshop when Michael and Kieran arrived for work.

'You're here early,' declared Michael. 'What happened, d'ja wet the bed?'

'That's enough cheek out of you. Where's Katie?'

'She works at her other job in Tamworth today and the rest of the week. So, you'll just have to deal with Kieran and me.'

The old mechanic turned to Kieran. 'What say I toss you for who goes for the lunches?'

'Okay, heads I win, tails you lose!'

'Boy, you're both sparkin' on all eight cylinders this morning.'

Michael added, 'When Katie's not here, it's usually the one who's least busy.'

'That sounds like a good solution.'

The old mechanic turned on the jug and prepared his morning cuppa. The two younger mechanics joined him.

'I was thinking about your Norton last night.'

'I think we all were,' informed Michael.

'I wasn't,' declared Kieran.

Ignoring Kieran's remark, Michael continued, 'Katie doesn't want me to get rid of it.'

'Really?' asked the old mechanic surprised.

'Yeah, she said she has a sentimental attachment to it.'

'You both had some good times on that old bike.'

'But that doesn't solve the problem of how we fund the purchase of one to restore.'

'How're your finances?' asked the old mechanic.

'Pretty tight! We're trying to save enough to meet our mortgage repayments during the quieter months, and in case interest rates go up.'

It had been a long time since the old mechanic had had to worry about mortgage payments, let alone all of the other costs associated with setting up a home, while at the same time, running a business. It was a sad reality of life that it takes money to make money.

'Anyway,' continued Michael, 'we've got work to do. Kieran, you can start on the Tiger; it needs a service. George, the owner of the Sunbeam says she's having drive problems, but she isn't sure if it's the clutch or the driveshaft.'

'She! Hmm, well I hope for her sake it isn't the shaft, 'cos it'll be expensive to repair if it is.'

The Sunbeam motorcycle was unusual for a British made machine of the era. There were three things that stood out: firstly, the engine was an overhead camshaft design (as opposed to the more common overhead valve); secondly, it was an in-line twin (instead of an opposed, parallel or V-twin); and third, it was shaft driven (rather than chain drive). While some of these features are now *de rigueur* in modern motorcycles, especially BMWs, in the years after WWII in Britain, they were unique.

Furthermore, while most shaft driven motorcycles commonly used bevel-driven gears, the Sunbeam makers did not want their machines to be mistaken for the German BMW, so they opted to use worm-drive gears. This proved to be the Achilles heel of the design, as the worm-drive gears were prone to stripping under power.

This particular motorcycle was a pale green Sunbeam S7 deluxe manufactured in 1950; and it was in showroom condition. The machine had been restored by an enthusiast in Adelaide and sold to the middle-aged owner from Armidale. She was taking it out for her maiden ride with the Armidale Vintage and Veteran Motorcycle Club when she suffered the ignominy of it breaking down. A club member recommended the old mechanic.

The Sunbeam started readily enough, but when he snicked it into first gear and eased out the clutch, the engine revved, but there was no motive power to propel the machine forward. The old mechanic listened to hear if there were any graunching noises of gears not properly meshing. Instead, there was a high piercing squeal that altered its note when the clutch lever was pulled in.

'That's a good sign,' he muttered to himself, 'I think!'

'Do you know what's wrong with it?' asked Michael from behind the rear of the Ariel he was working on.

'It's the clutch; but whether it's an easy fix or not, I'll reserve judgement.'

'The owner wanted me to contact her before we did anything major.'

'I won't know if major work's required until I investigate further. The squealing noise's caused by the clutch race – it's probably dry and either wearing or worn out. If I can get to the race and remove it, it's a quick and easy job.'

'And if you can't?'

'I'll need to remove the gearbox, and to get to the gearbox, I need to remove the engine. Let's just hope I can get the race out.'

As Michael turned his attention back to the job at hand, he realised there was still much he needed to learn about classic British motorcycles, especially those that were out of the norm, and with problems out of the ordinary.

The lady owner was fortunate in that the old mechanic was able to extract the bearing race without too much difficulty. An inspection of the bearings revealed that the three balls needed to be replaced. Once that was done, he repacked them in grease and reinstalled them in the clutch. By morning tea time he was taking the Sunbeam for a test ride.

When he had parked the Sunbeam, the old mechanic joined the two younger mechanics for smoko.

'That's the first Sunbeam I've seen in here for ages,' stated Michael.

'Yeah, you don't see many around,' said the old mechanic.

'How did you know what was wrong with it, and how did you know how to fix it?'

'Certain bikes have certain things that can go wrong. While some problems are generic, like poor tune, worn wheel bearings or brakes, other things are specific to particular bikes. For the Sunbeam, when it won't go, it's either the drive-shaft or it's the clutch. I just happened to remember that, if it's the clutch, then it's probably because the bearing race's dry and/or needing adjustment.'

Michael shook his head in amazement.

'Don't worry Mike, when you're my age and you've been doing this for 50 years or more, you'll know all there is to know too.'

'That's a scary thought.'

'I don't think I'll be doin' this in 50 years,' advised Kieran.

'What're gonna be doin' instead?' asked the old mechanic.

'I dunno; Lilly wants to get a farm.'

'I can just imagine you riding a horse into the sunset.'

'Huh, I'll be ridin' a motorbike.'

'What about you Mike; what'll you be doin' in 50 years?'

'You remember the saying George, "find a job you love and you'll never work a day in your life". I love doin' what I'm doin'; I see no point in gettin' another job where I hafta work. Now, speaking of work, what've you got on, Kieran?'

'I finished the Tiger. Dya want me ta start on the Beeza?'

'Okay, and George, the owner of the Ajay's having trouble starting it. He thinks it's electrical, but he's not sure.'

'Okay.'

Michael went back to the Ariel that he was working on, but a few minutes later, he was surprised when the old mechanic approached him. 'Can we talk?'

'Sure, what's up?'

'Outside.'

Michael followed the old mechanic out of the workshop, unsure of what to expect from his father-in-law. He rephrased the question, 'Is something wrong?'

'No, nothing's wrong. I just wanted to put a proposal to you on your own.'

'What proposal?'

'I've been thinking about your plan for me to restore a classic bike.'

'Is there a problem with that?'

'Well, as far as I can tell, the only flaw to the plan is you don't have any seed funding.'

'What do you mean?'

'Funds to get the plan off the ground. Once we get to the point of selling and then buying the next one, it should be self supporting. But we need the funds to start. Right?'

'Yeah, that's why I planned to sell my Norton,' said Michael, who was beginning to feel exasperated.

'Well, what if I was to put up the cash?'

'Do you have that sort of money?'

'I've still got some left over from the sale of the Vincent.'

'But that's your retirement money.'

'In case you hadn't noticed Mike, I ain't retired.'

'Um, I don't know.'

'Mike, it'll only be a loan; you can pay me back when we sell the bike. And besides, you're the one who said you didn't want to see an opportunity go begging.'

'I suppose it does make sense.'

'Of course it makes sense.'

'Can I check to see what Katie thinks?'

'She doesn't need to know. I just want it to be between you and me.'

'But she'll find out anyway.'

'Yes, but by then it'll be too late for her to say anything.'

'Okay, well let me think about it.'

Now it was the old mechanic's turn to feel exasperated, but he held his peace and went back inside the workshop to resume work on the AJS.

Nothing more was said for the remainder of the day. The old mechanic did not wish to labour the point, so he decided to proceed with the plan regardless of what Michael would decide. He came to the conclusion that it was easier to seek forgiveness than it was to get approval.

That evening, after dinner, he again turned on his laptop and began searching for a suitable motorcycle to restore. He pored over dozens of pages of advertisements, before settling on a 1948 Vincent Comet 500 in pieces.

Vincents, and especially the 1000cc V-twins, command a premium over the average classic British motorcycle. While the Comet was nowhere near as expensive to buy, they were still at the higher end of the market. To purchase a restored Vincent Comet, a buyer could expect to pay between $20,000 and $30,000 compared to between $10,000 and $15,000 for a Norton ES2 of the same vintage and condition.

The old mechanic believed that the owner of this particular Comet either did not know what it was worth, or had discovered something wrong with the motorcycle and was not letting on. He rang the number. An old lady answered.

'*Hello.*'

'Hello, I'm enquiring about the motorcycle you have for sale.'

'*Yes.*'

'Is the bike complete?'

'*Um, I think so ... my late husband was going to restore it, but ... he past away before he could finish it.*'

'I'm very sorry to hear that.'

'*That's alright dear, we all have to go some time ... do you ride a classic motorbike.*'

'Yes, I have a Norton Dominator.'

'*My Jack had a Norton once ... and an Ariel ... but he always wanted a Vincent.*'

'They're a lovely motorcycle.'
'*Do you know how to restore motorbikes?*'
'Yes, I'm a motorcycle mechanic.'
'*My Jack was a mechanic … do you want to buy it?*'
'That's why I'm calling.'
'*Well, you can have it on one condition.*'
'And what's that?'
'*You have to promise me that, when you've finished, you'll take it to Jack's grave so he can see it.*'
'I'm sure that won't be a problem … How much do you want for it?'
'*$5000.*'
'Really? $5,000 … you know you could get a lot more than that.'
'*Oh I know that dear, but I don't need the money, and you seem to be a very nice man.*'

The old mechanic hung up the phone with the vague notion that he was taking advantage of the old lady. But before he could dwell any further on the matter, the telephone rang.

'Hello.'
'*Hi George, it's Michael.*'
'Hi Mike.'
'*Um, about the money …*'
'Before you say anything, I've already spent it.'
'*You have? Whad'ja buy?*'
'A 1948 Vincent Comet.'
'*Wow, how much was that?*'
'About half of what it should have been … I'll tell you about it in the morning … Goodnight!'

## Chapter 5

# THE NEXT CHAPTER

The old mechanic rose early the following morning, feeling as excited as a small boy at Christmas. Even though the Vincent Comet that he had enquired about the previous evening was yet another old classic British motorcycle in urgent need of restoration, it was more than that to him. It marked the starting point of the next chapter in his long working life.

In spite of the assurance given by the old lady that the bike was complete, he had yet to come across a "basket case" that was what the vendor described. Still, that was part of the allure of restoring a classic motorcycle. Indeed, for many restorers, the quest to find that elusive part was just as important as putting all of the parts back together again. But for the old mechanic, the end state was what it was all about. The restoration was the means to the end, with the end being the sale for a profit and the purchase of the next one to restore.

The old lady lived in Guyra; a drive of about two hours north. She said she would prefer cash, so he would need to wait until the bank opened before he could withdraw the money. He was sipping his tea when the two younger mechanics arrived for work.

'Morning Mike; morning Kieran,' he called when they had removed their helmets.

'Morning George,' they replied in unison.

When the two younger men joined him for their morning cuppa, Michael said, 'So tell me about this bike you've just bought.'

'Well, as I mentioned last night, it's a 1948 Vincent Comet.'

'How much are you paying for it?'

'Five grand.'

'Five grand? Really? For a Vincent?' Michael's mouth was agape.

'It's a Comet, not a Rapide or a Black Shadow.'

'Yeah, wow! What condition's it in?'

'It's in pieces, so a "basket case", I assume.'

'Wherisit?' asked Kieran.

'Up at Guyra.'

'So, what're waitin' for?' asked Michael. 'I thought you'd be up there already.'

'The old lady wants cash, so I gotta wait for my bank to open.'

'They've got banks in Guyra, you know.'

'Yeah, but my account's here.'

'Doesn't matter; these days they're all linked electronically. You can go into any branch in the country and do almost any kinda transaction with your own money.'

'I hadn't thought of that. Okay, I'll leave at half seven; that way I'll be in Guyra just as they open.'

'Dya want one of us ta come with ya?' asked Kieran.

'No, I should be okay,' affirmed the old mechanic. 'It's in pieces, so it should be easy to load into the truck.'

'And besides,' Michael advised Kieran, 'we're got plenty to keep us busy here.' Then to the old mechanic he warned, 'Make sure you take the tarp, there's a storm forecast for this arvo.'

'With any luck, I'll be back before the storm.'

As luck would have it, the storm arrived early. The old mechanic was just leaving Uralla on the New England Highway on the return journey, when the front hit. The morning had been hot with a strong north-westerly wind blowing. But, to the southwest storm clouds were gathering. Towering cumulonimbus clouds changed colour from fluffy white to heavy grey with a menacing greenish tinge – a sure sign that they were heavy with hail.

The wind blast when the storm front hit rocked the truck such that the old mechanic struggled to keep driving on a straight trajectory. But when the rain started to fall, it did so by the bucket-load – it poured. Visibility became so poor that he had to slow to a crawl, and eventually, pull onto the side of the road and stop; the volume of water overwhelming the wiper's ability to clear the windscreen. And then the hail started. It was pea-sized at first, and then gradually increased to be the size of golf balls. There was little for him to do but wait for the storm to subside, and pray that the windscreen would not crack.

As so often happens, when torrential rain falls, some people do not have the good sense to pull over and wait the few minutes it would take for the storm front to pass. They continue on despite limited visibility and even more limited traction.

Aquaplaning occurs when a layer of water builds up between the vehicle tyre and the surface of the road. The higher the speed of the vehicle and the greater the volume of water on the road, the greater the likelihood that the tyre tread will be unable to disperse the water, causing the vehicle to aquaplane. When a vehicle is aquaplaning, it does not respond to any inputs from the driver; so, the brakes will not stop it, and the steering wheel will not turn it. The vehicle, to all intents and purposes, is out of control.

That is exactly what occurred about ten kilometres down the road from where the old mechanic had stopped for the storm. The driver of a Toyota Camry was travelling at the speed limit, but much too fast for the conditions. He struck a sheet of water on a curve of the single lane highway and ploughed straight on, into the path of a semi-trailer travelling in the opposite direction. The truck driver had nowhere to go; his rig jack-knifing as he tried to turn and brake to avoid the car. The two vehicles collided nearly head-on at a combined speed of around 180 kmh. The rig toppled over, spilling its load across both lanes of the highway. The truck driver escaped with minor injuries. The car driver died at the scene.

When the rain had subsided, the old mechanic resumed his journey home, only to stop again in the line of traffic at the scene of the accident. The emergency services had yet to arrive, and there was already a crowd gathered, offering whatever assistance they could. With no way past, he made a U-turn and returned to Uralla. He made a brief stop for lunch before taking a detour via Walcha for the trip home.

He arrived back at the workshop after the two younger mechanics had finished their lunch and had resumed working on customer bikes. They downed tools when the old mechanic drove slowly up the laneway. Michael greeted him as he parked the truck.

'What took ya so long? I was expecting you back two hours ago.'

'There was a big prang on the highway this side of Uralla. The road was blocked in both directions. I had to go back and detour through Walcha.'

'What 'appened?' asked Kieran.

'A head-on between a semi and a car; the car was a mess.'

'Did'ja stop?'

'No, there was already a crowd there. I didn't think I'd be able to do anything for the poor beggar, so I did a U-ie and went back to Uralla.'

Michael did not like talking about motor vehicle accidents, especially when one of the occupants was dead as a result, so he switched the conversation to the load on the back of the truck. 'Have you got the bike?'

'Of course.'

The three mechanics undid the ropes and pulled back the tarpaulin to reveal the Vincent Comet in pieces. Despite his best efforts to protect the contents of the tray, water had seeped under the cover and had soaked into the cardboard boxes. The old mechanic was just about to warn the others to take care lifting them, in case they fell apart, but he was too late. Kieran grasped the sides of a box containing engine parts, only to have the bottom fall out, spilling the contents into the truck tray.

'Be careful!' said the old mechanic.

'Sorry George.'

'Is it all there?' asked Michael.

'As far as I can tell, it is. But I won't know for sure until I start putting it back together.'

The three men unloaded the truck and placed the various parts on the bench inside the workshop. While Michael and Kieran returned to their individual tasks, the old mechanic went through the boxes, sorting their contents.

The previous owner had already repainted, rechromed or polished, as necessary, all of the cycle parts and had made a start on reassembling the motor. The wheels still needed work, and the old tyres needed to be replaced. The Amal carburettor appeared to be original, meaning it would require a refurbishment kit to ensure the perishables were renewed. Otherwise, the motorcycle appeared to be complete, as the old lady claimed.

By mid-afternoon, the old mechanic had ordered the new carbie kit, new spokes for the wheels, and new tyres. In the six months since he had restored the Vincent Black Shadow, he had discovered an alternate source, in Australia, of 20- and 21-inch tyres that would suit the peculiar wheel sizes of this motorcycle. While he would have changed to an 18- and 19-inch wheel combination if he was restoring the Comet for himself, he decided to retain the standard wheel sizes for the machines that he would be restoring. It certainly helped that the Vincent rims were still in good condition.

'You comin' over for smoko George?' called Kieran.

'Yeah, in a sec.'

When the old mechanic finally joined the two younger men, they were already drinking their beverage of choice.

'What are you two doin' this weekend?' asked the old mechanic as he waited for his tea to draw.

'My neighbour's asked me to help him sort out his Triumph Bonneville,' advised Michael.

The old mechanic looked at his son-in-law. 'That's unusual for you to be moonlighting,' he teased.

'Yeah, I know, but I felt obligated. Besides, it always helps to be on the good side with your neighbours. You never know when you might need a favour in return.'

'Is it a new Bonneville, or an old one?'

'It's one of those new Bonnevilles made to look old.'

'What's he wanna do to it?'

'The same as everyone wants: more power and better handling. Um, why do they call it moonlighting?'

'Back in the day, when everyone worked during daylight hours, if you had a second job, it had to be at night, during the hours of moonlight. So, if you were moonlighting, it meant you were working a second job.'

'Oh, I see.'

'What about you Kieran, you goin' out with Lilly on the weekend?'

'Me baptism's on Sund'y.'

'Oh, gee, I almost forgot. What time's the service start?'

'It's at two in the afternoon, at the Riverside Park.'

'How come it's in the park?'

'Our church yuzh'ly meets in a school 'all. We ain't got a pool, so we go ta the river for baptisms, just like in Jesus' time.'

'Is anyone from your family goin'?'

'Me mum said she'll be there. Dad reck'ns 'e only goes ta church for weddin's 'n fune'rals.'

The old mechanic turned to Michael. 'You goin' Mike?'

'I hadn't planned to.'

'I'd be good support for Kieran, and besides, you might even learn somethin'.'

'Hmm, I dunno. I'll ask Katie; if she wants to go, I'll go too.'

'I'm sure it'd be good for all of us.'

# Chapter 6

# THE LIFE OF RILEY

The weekend was the only opportunity during the week that Katie and Michael had time to spend together on their own to complete the housework, go shopping, or indulge in a sleep-in. So, they only gave up this precious time begrudgingly. Jim, for his part, was acutely aware that Michael was giving up his down-time at no cost, to assist him with the modifications to his Triumph.

The new Triumph Bonneville T100s are essentially a styling exercise. While extremely popular amongst older riders, the bikes pay mere "lip-service" to the original Triumphs of the 1950s and 60s that broke motorcycle land speed records on the Bonneville Salt Flats in the USA.

While the average rider would be mostly satisfied with the handling and performance of the standard machine, those raised on a diet of more sport-oriented machinery might feel let down. Thankfully, there are a large number of after-market suppliers available to provide the necessary items to improve both the performance and the handling of the standard motorcycle. Jim had researched extensively and had purchased the items he thought he would need to overcome the deficiencies of his Bonneville.

On bumpy and twisty roads, which are the norm for country NSW, the front forks of the T100 rapidly run out of initial travel with little in the way of compression or rebound damping. While the springs are progressive – meaning that they are wound at different rates in order to offer a soft initial action before getting progressively harder to compress as the spring compresses further – overall they are too soft. At the rear of the bike, the shock absorbers feel at odds with the front in that the springs feel overly hard. They also feel like there is little in the way of damping so that when the bike hits a bump, the rear end continues to bounce like a pogo-stick.

The sporting version of the Triumph Bonneville, the Thruxton, uses a smaller diameter front wheel – 18-inch rather than 19-inch – and rear shock absorbers that are 20 mm longer. So, the Thruxton, which uses the same frame, has both more ground clearance, because the rear end is higher, and quicker steering, because the forks are at a steeper angle. The shocks from the Thruxton are an easy fit for the Bonneville, and have the added bonus of using heavier weight oil providing improved damping. Jim was able to fit the pair of replacement shock absorbers from after-market supplier Ikon himself, but he needed assistance with the forks.

'I really appreciate your help with this,' he said as Michael began to remove the forks from the triple clamps of the T100.

'Don't thank me now; wait 'til we're finished.'

'How did you come to be a motorcycle mechanic?'

'It was almost by accident, really. I had a Triumph Thunderbird that needed some work and called in to see my local bike mechanic. I needed a job and he needed someone to help in the workshop. I became his apprentice the following year.'

'Do ya like it?'

'Like it? I love it. There isn't a job in the world I can think of that I'd rather be doin'.'

'I never liked workin' on bikes much. I preferred to spend my time ridin' 'em. My ol' man was always workin' on his bikes; he never seemed to have much time to ride.'

'What bikes did he have?'

'Old pommy ones that leaked oil all over the place, Beezas and Trumpies mostly.'

'You can make them oil tight, if you know what to do. My bike doesn't leak.'

With new heavier K-Tech springs in the fork tubes, new valves, a pair of Thruxton pre-load adjusters and 20-weight oil, the Bonneville now had front forks to match the new rear shock absorbers. In less than three hours, the two men had completed the suspenders on the Bonneville.

'That was easier than I thought,' suggested Jim.

'Yeah, sometimes a job that you think is gonna be hard is easy, and sometimes a job you think is gonna be easy is hard,' replied Michael.

'I'd rather have the first type.'

'Me too!'

To provide better access to replace the two rear shock absorbers, Jim had already removed the standard twin mufflers. He had purchased a pair of slip-on Staintune Reverse Cone stainless steel mufflers in their place and these were the next to be fitted. Besides weighing slightly less than the original fitment items, they were said to produce as much as 8 horsepower more with improved throttle response, as well as a boost to mid-range torque, without the need for further modifications.

While Jim could have gone the "whole hog" and made changes to the air box, air filters and air injection, as he had initially planned, these would have necessitated a change to the ECU mapping, which needed to be done with the aid of a dynamometer in a motorcycle workshop at greater cost. Michael suggested that he should try the bike as it was to see if he was happy with it, before going to significant further effort and expense.

When the two men had completed their work, Michael ordered, 'Wheel it out and start it up, I wanna hear how loud the new pipes are.'

Obediently, Jim grasped the handlebars of the motorcycle and pushed it out of his garage, turned the key and thumbed the starter. The exhaust gave an initial bark, before settling into a deep burble as the engine idled.

'Rev it a bit.'

Jim twisted the throttle several times; each time the new pipes gave a satisfying bark.

'Gee that sounds nice,' stated Michael.

'Yeah, and with the promise of better performance, if the website's anything to be believed,' asserted Jim. 'Would'ja like to come for a ride – I promise I'll take things easy so you can keep up.'

Michael ignored the implied insult, but declined the invitation anyway. 'Nah, I can't; I promised Katie I'd give her a hand with the housework when we finished.'

'Ah, the joys of married life.'

Michael thought about making a smart remark in reply, but all the terms he could think of were crude, so instead he just said, 'Enjoy the ride.'

'Well, thanks very much for your help Mike, I owe you one,' said Jim.

'Just one?'

By the time Jim had tidied up, washed his hands, changed his clothes and donned his jacket, helmet and gloves, it was getting late. Thankfully, with daylight saving still in operation, the sun would not set until almost 8:00 pm. That still gave him several hours of play time.

The New England Highway is heavily policed, especially on weekends during the summer months, so anyone who wants to have a decent "fang", whether by car or motorcycle, usually sticks to the back roads. The most entertaining roads, especially for motorcyclists, are those that follow the local creeks and rivers as they meander through the countryside; roads like the one from Tamworth to Nundle. From Nundle, there are two choices: Crawney Road or Lindsays Gap Road. After a brief section of highway to Wallabadah, the return journey takes the rider through Quirindi and Werris Creek.

Jim's Triumph Bonneville was everything he had hoped for, and more. The improved throttle response and additional mid-range torque the engine now made added to the enjoyment of the ride. The bike accelerated cleanly out of tight corners and raced into the upper reaches of the rev range on the straights. Where there was a succession of tight corners, he could leave the bike in a higher gear and use the fatter torque curve to power out of each bend.

But it was the modifications made to the suspension that really transformed the bike. No longer did it run wide on corners, and he had much more confidence with the front end, meaning he could enter tight corners at higher speeds than previously. And now that there was a better match between the forks and the rear shocks, there was less pitching and the overall ride quality was much improved. Even though the bike had increased ground clearance, Jim could still scrape the footpegs. As he feared, the limiting factor with the machine's handling was now the tyres, so next time, he decided, he would go for a stickier compound.

As he turned on to the highway for the run up to Wallabadah, he thought about the additional modifications to the engine he had planned. While he was a firm believer in the adage that "too much power was never enough", he also realised that the small increase in power he would gain would be matched by an exponential increase in the cost. Even though the new exhaust pipes had cost him over a thousand dollars, he considered they were still a cheap way of making horsepower. Further modifications would cost a great deal more money than that, for not that much more increase in power.

Turning off the highway to Quirindi, he put his thoughts aside while he concentrated on the road. Wallabadah Road loosely follows Quirindi Creek through mostly farming country. The day was fast ending and, by the time he arrived in the township of Quirindi, he was beginning to get hungry. As he rode slowly up the main street, he noticed a bevy of motorcycles, mostly Harley Davidsons, parked outside the Commercial Hotel. He pulled up and manoeuvred his bike next to an old classic Norton.

Before he entered the hotel, he took a close look at the Norton. It was a twin in very good condition. The motor was still hot, so its rider had not arrived long before he did. Jim entered the noisy bistro and surveyed the sea of faces. The Harley riders were easy to identify: big and burley, with beards, tattoos and black t-shirts.

At a table in the corner sat an elderly grey-haired fellow. On the seat next to him were a Belstaff jacket and an open-faced helmet with a pair of flying goggles attached. After Jim bought a schooner of bitter and ordered a steak sandwich, he went straight to the man's table.

'Are you on your own?' asked Jim.

'Yeah, unless you wanna join me,' replied the old mechanic.

When Jim had taken off his jacket and placed his helmet on the floor, he sat down. 'Is that your Norton parked out the front?'

'Yeah, that's my Dommie. Why do you ask?'

'Ya just don't see many like that around. Did you restore it yourself?'

'No, I bought it like that. I do restore bikes, but not that one. What do you ride?'

'I've got a Bonneville T100 – a new classic, rather than an old one.'

'D'ya like it?'

'I do now. I've just upgraded the suspension and put new exhaust pipes on it. So, it now goes and handles like it was always supposed to.'

It did not take the old mechanic long to realise that the man he was speaking to was Katie and Michael's neighbour, but he did not say anything to Jim. He was just about to speak when his number was called. When he had collected his meal, he returned to the table and sat down.

'My name's George Edwards, what's yours?'

'Jim Browning.'

The two men shook hands.

'You retired Jim, or are you still workin'?'

'I was made redundant a coupla months ago, so yeah, I'm retired. What about you?'

'I tried to retire, but I got too bored. So, I went back to work last week.'

'What do you do?'

The old mechanic was about to tell Jim he was a motorcycle mechanic but, he thought, sometimes a little information is too much. 'I'm a mechanic. What did you do before you were made redundant?'

'I was Workshop Foreman at Redscape Manufacturing, but I'm a fitter and turner by trade.'

'Do you like being retired?'

'I live the life of Riley; I get up when I want, go to bed when I want, eat, sleep, and ride my bike as much as I want. What's not to like?'

'D'ya miss people?'

'No, not much. I still get to meet people, and I've got some really nice neighbours.'

'You still married?'

'Nah, me missus shot through when I stopped work. What about you?'

'She died some years back.'

'I'm sorry.'

'That's alright, it's not your fault. But I've still got a daughter, and a new son-in-law. And pretty soon I hope to have grandkids.'

'Where do they live?'

The old mechanic took a big mouthful of food so that he did not have to answer right away. As he chewed his food, he wondered whether he should tell Jim or not. Eventually he decided to tell the truth.

'Banjo Creek; in fact, I think they may even be your next-door neighbours.'

Jim pondered his dinner companion's answer before replying, 'You mean Katie and Michael?'

'Yeah, Katie's my daughter.'

'They don't quite live next door, but close enough. Gee, so you're a motorcycle mechanic and Michael works for you.'

'Not any more. Now I work for him.'

'Wow, what a small world.'

'Yep, it sure is.'

## Chapter 7

## WALKING THE WALK

The old mechanic had never been to an open-air baptism before. Indeed, in all his 65 years, he had never previously been to the baptism of an adult. Having been brought up Anglican, he had been christened as an infant and confirmed as a teenager. He and his wife had Katie christened when she was about three months old, even though by that stage they had ceased going to church themselves. So, he approached Kieran's baptism with a good deal of curiosity, wondering how different the service would be compared to his own past experiences. It would turn out to be unlike any church service he had ever been to.

Katie could count on both hands the number of times she had been to church. These were: her own christening, of which she had no memory; the two funerals, her mother's and Kevin's; three weddings, including her own; and the four times as part of her nuptial preparations. Michael was about on par with Katie, except he had not been christened. And like the old mechanic, neither had ever been to an open-air service.

Katie was excited about going, Michael less so. Kieran had suggested that they dress casually, which, in Australia, could mean anything from slacks and a collared and buttoned shirt, to shorts and a t-shirt. They all decided to err on the side of caution and wore jeans and a collared short-sleeve shirt – or in Katie's case, a blouse – with hats and sunglasses all 'round. Katie and Michael picked up the old mechanic on the way.

'D'ya know anything about this church that Kieran's involved with?' asked the old mechanic as Michael manoeuvred the car back onto the highway for the run up to Tamworth.

'Nah, he hasn't said much about it,' replied Michael.

'Has Lilly said anything to you Katie?'

'Only that it's contemporary, and there're lots of young people. She's invited me to come, but I said I'd take a rain-check.'

'It's not one of those "happy-clappy" Pentecostal types is it?'

'I don't know,' professed Katie, 'but I don't think so.'

'Well, I suppose we'll find out soon enough.'

The car-park was already filling up when they arrived. The Riverside Park was a popular spot for families to relax and enjoy a summer Sunday picnic or barbecue. At one end of the park, a group was engaged in a game of "back-yard cricket", while at the other end, frisbees were flying here and there. At the river's edge, was a group of about 60 people, seated mostly on folding chairs and picnic rugs. Katie recognised Lilly and Kieran in the midst of the crowd; Lilly saw her at about the same time.

Kieran was relieved to see his work friends arrive. He was clearly a little nervous as he introduced them to his mother. Lilly then introduced the three of them to her parents.

'So, you're Kieran's boss,' Lilly's father declared sneeringly to the old mechanic.

'No, I used to be, Michael's his boss now.'

'But you're a motorcycle mechanic,' he iterated distastefully as if it was the worst possible type of occupation.

The old mechanic could see where this conversation was heading and decided to change its direction. 'I'm a lot of things, but yes, I'm a motorcycle mechanic. But I'm also a father, a father-in-law, and hopefully, one day a grandfather. Once I was a husband, but sadly, no more. What do you do?'

'Um, ah, I'm an accountant.'

The old mechanic had clearly made Lilly's father flustered by his reply, but he was determined not to become the target of this sad individual's petty prejudices.

The old mechanic continued. 'Kieran's a good lad, and an excellent mechanic. He's also very smart; in fact, I think he's got the brains to achieve almost anything he sets his mind to.'

Lilly's father had not expected this kind of praise about his daughter's boyfriend. He had done everything he could to discourage Lilly from going out with Kieran in the early stages, even banning her from being carried as pillion on his motorcycle, all to no avail. He had had high hopes of marrying her off to a lawyer or a doctor or some such professional, not some "grubby grease-monkey", as he had described him to her.

But one thing that Lilly had acquired from her mother was a stubborn streak; once she had set her mind to do something, nothing would change it. The more her father had said no to her about Kieran, the more determined she was to change his mind and, so that he would eventually allow her to marry him. Getting Kieran to come to church and become a Christian, was the biggest hurdle to overcome; in her mind, the only one.

A small band started to play and the congregation stood and began singing some modern hymns that almost everyone else seemed to know. Lilly passed some sheets of paper with the song words to Katie, who shared them with Michael and her father. They were not familiar with the tunes, but enjoyed the congregational singing just the same.

After three songs, a man who was standing at the front of the congregation nearest the river bank motioned everyone to be seated. He was casually dressed like the rest of the congregation; it was only later that the old mechanic was informed that he was one of the pastors. After saying a prayer and welcoming everyone, and especially the friends and family of those being baptised, he invited the candidates to join him at the front.

Another man, who turned out to be the senior pastor, then stood up and addressed the congregation in a loud clear voice: 'Baptism is an important milestone in the life of a Christian. It marks the time when you are saying to the world that you now belong to Jesus. But there is nothing magical about the waters of baptism; the water is still the Peel River and it still tastes disgusting.'

Everyone chuckled at the pastor's attempt at humour.

'Going through the waters of Christian baptism, no sooner makes you a Christian, than going through a car-wash makes you a car.'

Everyone chuckled again, some even laughed. When they had settled down, he continued.

'And there's nothing magical about the words I utter; there's no change in the person after they've been baptised. They're still the same people as before. But if that's the case, you may ask, why then do we baptise? Well, there are three reasons.' He went on to talk about the meaning of baptism and its purpose.

The sun was beating down on the people gathered on the river bank. Those unfamiliar with church quickly became bored with the proceedings. Many of the children started fidgeting; some even decided that they would rather join in with the other children playing games. The longer the minister spoke, the more restless they became.

Both the old mechanic and Michael began to wonder if they had made the right decision to come, though for different reasons. As the minister continued, the old mechanic thought back to the time when he and his late wife were regular church goers. While the people were more or less the same, the message from the senior pastor was different. The more he spoke, the more uncomfortable he felt. Michael also felt uncomfortable, but it had more to do with the hot sun than with what was being said.

Eventually, the minister realised that he needed to cut his sermon short. But he still had something important to say: 'Some people call what we do "Believer's Baptism", but I have to disagree with them. We can't see into the hearts of those who come to us to be baptised. The best that we can do is to determine whether they have a "credible profession of faith". The elders watch and observe how they behave, and listen to how they speak, and we interview those who know them well. Only once we're satisfied that they "walk the walk", as well as "talk the talk", do we baptise them. We've done that and we're satisfied that those who are to be baptised here today are what they profess to be.

'I'd now like to invite Hannah, Rachael, Marc and Kieran to come forward to be baptised.'

While the four young people stood up and joined the senior pastor at the river's edge, the band began to play again, signalling that it was time for another song. The congregation stood to sing while the senior pastor and the four candidates stepped into the water.

The slow-moving Peel River was murky and the river bottom was thick with fine silt. The five people in the water had to take care as their feet sank deep into the mud with each step. When they were all at about waist deep, at the end of the song, the senior pastor prayed again, speaking loudly so that all could hear. Then he said, 'Do you Hannah, Rachael, Marc and Kieran desire to be baptised?'

They all replied, 'We do.'

'Relying on God's grace, do you promise to love God with your whole being and to love your neighbour as yourselves?'

'We do.'

'Do you renounce evil and its power in the world, which defies righteousness and separates you from the love of God?'

'We do.'

'Do you turn to Jesus Christ, accepting him as your Lord and Saviour? And do you intend to be Christ's faithful disciple, obeying his word, and showing his love, to your life's end?'

'We do.'

Addressing the congregation, the senior pastor asked, 'Do you promise to pray for, teach, guide and nurture these four young people to be imitators of Christ?'

The congregation responded, 'We do.'

The senior pastor, taking each candidate in turn, baptised by fully immersing them with water while uttering these words, 'I baptise you in the name of the Father, and of the Son, and of the Holy Spirit.'

Each time the congregation responded, 'Amen.'

After praying a third time and uttering the benediction, the senior pastor shepherded the four young people toward the river bank while the band played and the congregation stood to sing one last song.

Kieran emerged from the water, as did his three companions, dripping wet. At Lilly's suggestion, he had worn a pair of swimming trunks underneath his clothes, and had brought a spare set of clothes to change into. She met him with a towel and a kiss in front of everyone. While it was no secret that they were "an item", it was also no secret that her father did not approve of the relationship. With his baptism out of the way, Lilly decided to make a public declaration that Kieran was now hers, and nothing anyone, including her father, could do or say would be able to change that.

With the service over, the old mechanic, Katie and Michael approached the spot where Kieran was drying his hair and upper body, with Lilly holding his discarded wet shirt. Members of the congregation, in small groups and individually, milled around to congratulate and speak with him. While the old mechanic waited his turn, the senior pastor approached him.

'Are you Kieran's dad?' he asked.

'Oh no, I'm his colleague, George Edwards,' replied the old mechanic.

As they shook hands, the senior pastor stated, 'So you're a "bikie" too.'

'I ride a motorcycle, but I'm not a bikie; not in the sense that you mean. Lumping all motorcycle riders in together is like lumping all Christians in together. We're all different, just like you lot are.'

'So, you're not a Christian then?'

'I didn't say that, but no, I stopped believing at about the same time you lot did.'

'We're not all the same you know. I never stopped believing.'

'Yeah well, what did you call it, a "credible profession"? First let me see if you "walk the walk", as well as "talk the talk"; then I'll believe you.'

# Chapter 8

# IN THE CLUB

With all the excitement of the baptism, and the heat of the afternoon summer sunshine, Katie and Michael arrived home feeling tired and a little the worse for wear. While they had worn protection against sunburn – sun-screen, hats and sunglasses – a shortage of fresh water to drink left them both feeling slightly dehydrated. Katie went to bed soon after their evening meal feeling a little nauseous, which she put down to too much sun. She awoke the next morning feeling worse.

As she lay in bed, she turned her head to the side; Michael was still sleeping soundly, his chest rising and falling rhythmically with each breath. The bedside clock told her it was just before 5:00 am. All of a sudden, she felt sick. She dashed from her bed to the bathroom, just in time. The sound of her vomiting woke Michael; he met her as she emerged wiping her face on a handtowel.

'Are you okay?' he asked, all concerned.

'I think so,' she lied.

Her face was pale in the early morning light. With the brightness of the bathroom lighting behind her, the nightie she was wearing was all but see through. But Michael was more concerned for her health than the sight of her almost naked body in silhouette.

'I think you should stay home today,' he said.

'I'll be alright, truly.'

Another wave of nausea swept over her and she raced back to the bathroom. When she emerged for the second time,

Michael met her with a large glass of electrolytes mixed with iced water.

'Here, drink this. It might not make you feel any better, but it shouldn't make you feel any worse.'

She drank the lemon flavoured liquid in one go.

'Thanks! I probably should've had a glass of that last night before I went to bed. I think I might've got a little too much sun yesterday.'

'Yeah, it was pretty warm,' said Michael, 'we both probably should've drunk some more fluids before we went to bed. But one thing you're definitely going to do today is you're staying home.'

Katie did not have the strength to argue. She sat on the edge of the bed suddenly feeling very tired. Lying back down, she fell fast asleep. When she woke again, it was fully light. The clock beside the bed said it was 9:37. The house was quiet. Michael must have gone to work, she thought.

Now ravenously hungry, she arose from her bed and went to the kitchen. After switching on the kettle, she took some crumpets from the freezer and popped them into the toaster. While they were cooking, she prepared a mug of strong coffee, and took a jar of honey and another of vegemite from the cupboard, and butter from the refrigerator. She felt so much better than she did earlier that morning.

With the heady aromas of honey and vegemite on hot crumpets and strong coffee, a wave of nausea swept over her once more. She raced back down the hall, only just making it to the bathroom before being sick yet again.

When she was fairly confident that she was not going to throw up any more, she telephoned her General Practitioner to see if she could get in to see her. Katie's timing was impeccable; someone else had cancelled just before she rang. She considered calling Michael to inform him of what she was doing, but decided against it as she did not wish to cause him undue further worry. After drinking another glass of electrolytes, she locked the unit and left for the doctors' surgery.

When the three mechanics had come together for their first cuppa of the day, the old mechanic realised that Katie was missing.

'Where's Katie?' he asked Michael.

'She was crook this morning. She thinks she might've got a bit too much sun yesterday, so I told her to stay home.'

'Just as long as that's all it was.'

'She was sleeping soundly when I left. I'll give her a ring later to make sure she's okay.'

Turning to Kieran, the old mechanic said, 'I had a good time yesterday, except for Lilly's old man. Gee, what is that guy's problem?'

'Yeah, I try an' keep outa 'is way if I can.'

'Yeah, I would too. Too bad *your* old man didn't wanna go. Whad'ja mum hafta say?'

'She said she enjoyed 'erself. She said she 'adn't been to church since she was a kid in Sund'y School. She reck'ned it's tot'ly diff'rent now.'

'Yep, it sure is. Whad'ju think of it Mike?'

'It was alright, except I didn't really understand what the guy in the water was talking about. Is that what your normal church services are like Kieran?'

'Yeah, 'cept the Bible talks yuzh'ly take 30 to 40 minutes and there's more of ev'rythin' else too.'

'Don't ya get bored?'

'No, it's int'restin', an' if I don' understan' anythin', Lilly 'elps me.'

'Is that all she helps you with?'

Kieran did not reply, although his face began to turn red. The old mechanic saw that as a sign that the topic needed changing.

'I went for a ride on Sat'd'y, blew the cobwebs out of me old Norton. When I stopped off at Quirindi, who do you think I met?'

'Who?' answered Michael and Kieran together.

'Your neighbour, the guy with the Bonneville.'

'Who, Jim?' asked Michael.

'Yeah, he was tellin' me how happy he was with the mods you made to his bike.'

'I really only worked on the forks; he'd already got the pipes and the rear shocks. I haven't seen him since; I'm glad he's pleased.'

'Yep, he sure is. So, what's on the plate for today Mike?'

'We've only got a few customer bikes in this morning. Kieran, you can start on the Norton Atlas – the owner says it's running like a dog, so it probably needs the carbies balanced, points cleaned up and the timing checked. George, you can start on the Comet you picked up on Friday, if you like?'

Getting an appointment to see a doctor at short notice in the country, even in a place as large as Tamworth, is difficult enough. Getting in to see a *female* doctor at short notice is nigh on impossible. Katie considered herself very fortunate.

The medical practice where Katie's doctor worked had a nursing sister whose job it was to vet the patients, take the vital signs of a patient before they entered the doctor's surgery. Besides being a more efficient use of the doctor's time, it tended to weed out the time-wasters; those who really only went to see the doctor because they were lonely and were looking for someone to talk to.

Katie's temperature, blood pressure and respiration were all normal. Her weight gave her a BMI (Body Mass Index) of 21.5, which was at the lower end of the normal range. Nothing could be deduced from the numbers alone. With a slip of paper with the details recorded, she returned to the waiting room to await her name being called. She did not have to wait long.

'Katie Edwards.'

Katie stood up and followed the doctor into the consultation room, gave her the slip of paper and sat down on the chair next to her desk.

'Hello Doctor Bailey.'

'Hello Katie,' said the doctor, 'what seems to be the trouble?'

'Well, yesterday, I spent the afternoon in the sun at Riverside Park, and last night I was feeling sick, so I went to bed early. Then this morning I was sick – I threw up three times. I think I might have got some sunstroke.'

'Hmm, tell me about the vomiting.'

Katie related the three episodes of her being sick that morning.

'Have you eaten anything since last evening?'

'No, I was preparing some crumpets for breakfast this morning, but the smell of them with the coffee made me sick again.'

'Hmm, are your periods regular?'

'Yeah, usually, but I'm a little bit overdue at the moment.' Katie went pale again as the blood drained from her face. 'You don't think I'm pregnant, do you?'

'There's only one way of finding out.'

The nursing sister tested a sample of her urine in her office while Katie waited nervously in the waiting room. When her name was called again, she jumped up and almost collided with another patient who was leaving.

When she was seated in the doctor's surgery, she asked, 'Is it good news or bad news?'

'That depends on your perspective. Do you want to have a baby?'

'Of course!'

'Then I suppose it's good news.'

Katie squealed with delight.

Michael had tried calling Katie during the mid-morning smoko break, but she did not answer her telephone. He left a voicemail message and asked her to call him back as soon as she had woken up. Katie had actually turned off her phone while she was in the doctor's surgery and had forgotten to turn it back on, so she did not get the message until later that afternoon.

A thousand and one thoughts flowed through her mind on the journey back from the surgery. The last time she had been pregnant, she had kept it a secret from everyone but her partner, only telling her father after the accident that had caused her to miscarry. She shuddered at the thought of something horrible happening again.

She and Michael had talked often about having children, but there had been a question mark over her fertility following the trauma, both physical and emotional, caused by the car crash that claimed her partner's life and the life of her unborn infant. While she had started using contraceptives once the two had become lovers, she had stopped taking the pill after they were married. So, the couple was hoping, rather than expecting, that Katie would fall pregnant again.

'Mikey's going to be so excited; I can't wait to tell him,' she said to herself.

Michael, for his part was beginning to get worried that he had not heard from his wife. He decided he would try her phone again during the lunch break and, if there was still no response, dash home to check on her. As it turned out, he did not need to be concerned.

Instead of going back to the unit at Banjo Creek, Katie continued on to the workshop. Just as Kieran was about to head off to the sandwich shop for the lunches, she drove up the laneway. Michael met her and opened the car door as she turned off the engine.

'Where've you been? I've been worried sick. Are you okay?' he asked as she stepped from the car.

Before he could say anything more, she threw her arms around his neck and gave him a long passionate kiss.

When she pulled back, he asked her again, 'Where've you been?'

Grasping his hand, she led him back inside the workshop saying, 'I'll tell you inside.'

The old mechanic joined Katie and Michael in the area where they normally had their lunch and smoko breaks.

When they were both seated, she announced, 'I went to see the doctor this morning.'

'What did he say?' asked Michael, concern written all over his face.

Katie was enjoying drawing her news out. '*She*, ran some tests and …'

'Come on Katie, tell us,' demanded her father.

'Yeah, come on Katie,' encouraged Michael.

'I'm pregnant.'

The news of her condition took some moments to sink in. But when it did, Michael leapt to his feet, yelling 'Woo hoo!' He then grasped Katie's hands, pulled her to her feet and the two of them started dancing in a circle.

All the old mechanic could say was, 'You little ripper.' He joined the other two in their dance, before hugging each of them in turn.

When Kieran returned with the lunches, he found all three talking excitedly.

'What's 'appenin?'

'Katie's in the club,' replied the old mechanic.

'Club? What club?'

'The puddin' club!'

Kieran gave a look that indicated he was none the wiser for the explanation.

'Katie's having a baby,' responded Michael. 'I'm gonna be a dad.'

# Chapter 9

# KEEPING YOUR MIND ON THE JOB

The news of Katie's pregnancy came as much of a surprise to Michael, just as it did to his wife. While he was aware that she had stopped taking contraceptives after they had returned from their honeymoon, he had not anticipated that she would fall pregnant so soon. The news, though greeted with great initial excitement, would mean significant changes for them both. It would also mean that they would have to manage for a time on just one income.

After the break for lunch, and the departure of Katie for home, the three men returned to their assigned tasks. Kieran had completed his work on the Norton Atlas and had started on a Royal Enfield Interceptor that had begun to blow smoke. Unless it was caused by leaking valve seals, then new piston rings and possibly reboring the cylinders would be in order, an outcome that would be both time consuming and costly.

The old mechanic was still sorting through the various parts of the Vincent Comet. While the previous owner had commenced rebuilding the motor, the old mechanic needed to satisfy himself that the work already carried out, had been done properly. Therefore, some of the restoration work, like the installation of bearings on the crankshaft, would have to be redone.

Michael started working on a 1954 BSA A10 Golden Flash 650, the first of the swinging arm frame models. The bike, which needed a new chain and drive sprockets, had an

Australian made Tilbrook sidecar attached. Having the sidecar attached made a difficult task that much more challenging.

Normally, when changing sprockets and chains, Michael would raise the whole bike on a scissor-lift. However, with the sidecar attached, the scissor-lift could not be used. Adding to the difficulty was that the sidecar was attached to the left-hand side of the motorcycle, the same side as the chain and sprockets, so access was an issue as well.

Michael had to make do with a portable hydraulic jack to raise the rear of the outfit to enable the back wheel to be removed. While earlier model A10s had a hinged rear mudguard that facilitated removal of the back wheel, the Birmingham Small Arms Company had deleted this feature for the 1954 model year. So, he would need to raise the bike much higher than he would a machine with the hinged mudguard.

While the Application of Safe Working Practices in an Automotive Environment was a discrete subject in their first year of study, workplace safety was a constant theme running through the entire apprenticeship course as the two younger mechanics completed both their theory and practical subjects at TAFE. So usually, every task they did in the workshop was completed with safety in mind, unless, of course, the mind was otherwise preoccupied.

As Michael jacked up the rear of the BSA, his mind was on how he and Katie would manage to keep the business operating, as well as pay their mortgage, when the baby arrived. Normally, when using the hydraulic jack, he would utilise a static jack-stand as insurance should the hydraulic jack fail. On this occasion, he forgot.

When he had raised the bike to the desired height, he unhooked the rear brake cable, loosened the rear axle nut and pushed the wheel forward so that he could release the chain from the rear sprocket. Once he had the chain off the sprocket, he pulled on the wheel to clear it from the swinging arm. As it came clear, the hydraulic jack collapsed.

Michael had positioned himself so that he was seated on the floor, with a leg on either side of the back wheel. When the jack collapsed, the wheel became jammed under the rear mudguard with the axel now sitting above the swingarm, while the lower arms connecting the sidecar to the motorcycle dropped down with a thud, pinning his left leg.

Michael cried out in pain.

The standard BSA A10 had a kerb weight of about 190 kg, but with a sidecar attached, the weight could be more than 300 kg. So when the jack collapsed, he had as much as half that weight on his leg.

The other two mechanics rushed to his aid. While Kieran lifted the rear of the outfit, the old mechanic dragged Michael clear.

'Crikey Mike,' said the old mechanic when he stood up and took in the scene, 'what are you doin' workin' without a jack stand?'

'Sorry George, ah, I forgot.'

He rolled up his left trouser leg to reveal a lump on his shin half the size of a tennis ball. Thankfully the skin had not broken, or worse.

'It's not like you to forget something important like that. What's up?'

'Nothing, I'll be okay. I just need to sit down for a bit. It must be nearly time for smoko anyway.'

The old mechanic helped his son-in-law to his feet. Michael hobbled over to a chair and sat down while Kieran moved a wooden stool closer so that he could rest his leg on it. From the freezer compartment of the refrigerator, the old mechanic took some ice and placed it in a zip-lock plastic bag. He then wrapped the bag in a clean cloth and instructed Michael to hold the bag on the lump.

'What's this for?' asked Michael.

'It should help get the swelling down. Is it sore?'

'Like you wouldn't believe.'

The old mechanic made tea for them both, while Kieran looked after himself. When he finally sat down with his mug, he asked Michael again, 'What's up? Are you worried about Katie?'

'About Katie, about the business, about how we're gonna pay the mortgage on one wage with another mouth to feed. Of course I'm bloody worried.' His bottom lip quivered as he stared into his mug of tea.

In all the time that Michael had been working for the old mechanic, he had never heard him swear. While he only occasionally cursed himself, hearing it from his son-in-law came as a shock. But he did not say anything; under the circumstances, he understood perfectly.

'Mike, I want you to be very clear about this: while ever I'm alive, I will *never* let you and Katie fail, even if it costs me every cent I own. Do you understand? I will never let you fail.'

Michael looked up into the face of his father-in-law before saying, 'I understand, but …'

'No buts about it Mike, do you understand?'

In a resigned tone he answered, 'Yeah … I understand.'

As the three men drank from their respective mugs, the old mechanic suggested, 'You were lucky, you know.'

'How so?' asked Michael as he checked the swelling of his leg.

'You were lucky it only crushed ya leg. If it hadn't been in the way, the wheel might've crushed ya family jewels.'

'Just as well Katie's 'avin' a baby already,' added Kieran.

Everyone laughed, despite the circumstances.

Michael was unable to continue working on the BSA Golden Flash, and incapable of riding his Norton, so he called Katie to come and pick him up to take him home. Naturally, she was very concerned for his welfare when he rang. She swung by in the car and drove him back to the unit in Banjo Creek.

The old mechanic took leave of the Comet and set to work on the outfit, while Kieran resumed his work on the Interceptor. He had already removed the head of the 736cc motor. An examination of the valve seats revealed that they had worn, so much so that oil was being drawn into the combustion chamber and burning, producing the bluish smoke. New hardened valve seats that were compatible with lead-free fuel would need to be ordered from their classic bike parts supplier. Being unable to do any more work on the Royal Enfield, he joined the old mechanic to assist him with the BSA.

'The owner of the In'erceptor's gettin' off lightly; I was 'alf expectin' a top-end rebuild: pistons, rings an' a rebore, at least,' advised Kieran.

'Yeah, I'll say,' replied the old mechanic. 'Didja check the bores to make sure they're okay?'

'Yeah, they're smooth as a baby's bum, as me ol' man sez.'

'You get on well with your dad, don't ya?'

'Yeah, 'e reckons we're more like best mates, than father an' son. D'you ever wish you'd 'ad a boy instead of a girl?'

The old mechanic stopped to think before answering. 'I wish we'd had both, but I'm happy to have had Katie. Besides, havin' a son-in-law like Mike, is like havin' a son anyway. And pretty soon with grandkids, I've got the best o' both worlds.'

Kieran continued, 'Lilly can't wait to 'ave kids. She says she wants a "quiver full", whatever that means.'

The old mechanic laughed. 'Don't ya know what a quiver full means?'

'Nah.'

'It's from the Bible.'

Kieran was none the wiser.

'You know what a quiver is?'

'Yeah, it's a thin' ya carry arro's in.'

'Well, if the arrows are children, a "quiver full" means lots of 'em. Do ya like kids?'

'Yeah, but I'm not sure if I wanna 'ouse full.'

'You mean a quiver full.'

Both men laughed.

'You like Lilly don't ya?' continued the old mechanic.

'Yeah, I can't imagine bein' with anyone else in the whole world.'

'Then why don't ya move in together?'

'We're Christians now; we don' believe in livin' together.'

'Then why don't ya get married?'

'We're plannin' to; we jus' 'avn't told anyone yet.'

Kieran's answer surprised the old mechanic, so much so that he dropped the ring-spanner he was using to loosen a nut holding the drive sprocket.

'Whad'ja say about keepin' yer mind on the job?' asked Kieran.

Suitably chastened, the old mechanic replied, 'Yeah, I know, but don't do as I do, do as I say.'

Kieran smiled, 'Me ol' man sez that too.'

Now that Katie knew the cause of her nausea, she was much more at ease. Having already been down this road once before, she knew how to manage the symptoms. Eating smaller portions more often and limiting foods that were oily, fatty or spicy, were usually enough to keep the vomiting at bay. She would also need to be increasing her intake of foods high in calcium and folate and, while she and Michael were only social drinkers, alcohol was now completely off the menu.

Michael's injury was of more immediate concern to her. While the swelling on his shin had gone down somewhat, his leg was still very painful, causing him to limp when he walked.

'I don't think you should be going to work tomorrow,' she said over dinner.

'But they need me,' argued Michael.

'They need you fit and well, is what they need. And besides, if you can't walk very well or ride a motorbike, what're you gonna do?'

'Supervise the others, making sure they keep their minds on the job.'

'What, like you were? I don't think either Kieran, or my father, need that much supervision.'

'Well, I could do the paperwork, ordering, invoices and stuff.'

'But that's my job,' pleaded Katie.

'Yeah, but you're having a baby.'

'Mikey, being pregnant doesn't mean that my life has to be put on hold for the next seven and a half months. I'm still capable of working. And besides, we need as much money as we can get for as long as we can get it.'

'So how long are you gonna work for?'

'For as long as I can.'

'But …'

Katie held up the palm of her hand to signal stop. 'You've got your work to do Mikey, and I've got mine. I'll make a deal with you: I won't stop you from doing yours, if you don't stop me from doing mine.'

'But you just said you didn't want me to go to work tomorrow.'

'But I'm not stopping you, your leg is.'

Michael smiled at the female logic before saying, 'I can't win, can I?'

'Nope!'

"Lo, children are an heritage of the LORD: and the fruit of the womb is his reward. As arrows are in the hand of a mighty man; so are children of the youth. Happy is the man that hath his quiver full of them: they shall not be ashamed, but they shall speak with the enemies in the gate." (Psalm 127:3-5 KJV)

# Chapter 10

## WHEN ONLY THE BEST WILL DO

The atmosphere in Lilly's home was becoming increasingly hostile. Her father had been shocked at the public display of affection when she kissed Kieran in front of the entire congregation after he emerged from the water following his baptism in the Peel River. When she arrived home from the service, he demanded that she break up with him.

Lilly's emotions were in turmoil. She loved Kieran; of that she was certain. But she also loved her parents and, being a Christian, she felt obligated to honour them. She considered that Kieran had done everything that he could possibly have done to win her father over: he stopped bringing his motorcycle around to pick her up, he started coming to church, he got converted, and now he had been baptised, but still her father was unhappy.

'You could do so much better Lillian,' he argued.

He always called her Lillian in times like this. She hated the name and thought it so old fashioned.

'But I don't want anyone else.'

'What about Duncan McKenzie? He's just finished his University degree and has a promising legal career ahead of him. And he comes from a good Christian family.' He emphasised the last part, hoping that would sway her.

'But he's so stuck up,' she countered.

'Well, what about young Stephen Davidson; he's going to be a doctor like his parents.'

'He's a creep.'

'Well, what about …'

Lilly interrupted him before he could continue, 'But I love Kieran. Don't you understand?'

She burst into tears and ran to her bedroom, slamming the door closed behind her.

Lilly's father turned to his wife, 'It's all your fault you know.'

'What did I do?' she pleaded.

'She's got that stubborn streak, like you have.'

'Well, I can't stop my genes from being passed on.'

'And you should have supported me right from the beginning.'

'Now you listen to me Alan Henderson. I did support you from the beginning. You said she couldn't go out on his motorbike. I agreed with you. You said Kieran had to come to church. I agreed. You said he had to become a Christian. I agreed. Those kids have done everything you wanted them to do, but you were never satisfied. You kept shifting the goalposts.'

'I never shifted the goalposts. My goal has always been to give Lillian the best life she can have. I just believe that she will be better off married to a university graduate, rather than some grubby grease-monkey.'

'You don't understand, do you?'

'Understand what?'

'The best life she can possibly have is to be married to the man she loves, and who loves her in return. What he does for a living is immaterial. If you truly want what's best for them, then you will give your blessing to their relationship.'

'Huh!'

'You were right, she is stubborn, just like I was when we started dating. Do you think my father was impressed when I started going out with a junior bank clerk?'

'Yes, but I was studying accountancy.'

'My father didn't care. He was short-sighted, like you are. His sole interest was how much money you earned.'

'So why did he allow us to get married?'

'Because my mother talked him round, just like I am now to you. Yes, Lilly's stubborn; I think she will marry Kieran with, or without, your consent. But how much better do you think it'd be if she knows that both of us have given them our blessing?'

Alan Henderson did not reply to his wife's question; it did not need a reply. She left him in the lounge room to think while she went to bed.

After some time, he arose from his chair and went to the bathroom. As he passed by Lilly's bedroom door, he noticed that the light was still on. He knocked. There was no answer. He turned the knob and pushed the door open.

He popped his head around the corner and asked, 'Can I come in Petal?'

Lilly was sitting up in bed with a book on her lap. Her eyes were puffy and her nose red. A half-empty box of tissues was on her bedside table. She pulled a tissue from the box and blew her nose while her father sat on the end of the bed.

'What're you reading?'

'A book.'

'Is it any good?'

'It's alright.'

'What's it about?'

'Christian love.'

'You know *I* love you, don't you?'

Lilly did not answer.

He continued, 'I've only ever wanted what's best.'

'Who for: for me, or for you?'

More tears flowed. She grabbed another tissue and blew her nose again.

The accusation had stung. He waited a few moments, searching for the right words to say before continuing.

'Do you really love him *that* much?'

'His name's Kieran dad, K-I-E-R-A-N, Kieran. And yes, of course I love him. I love him more than anyone or anything in the whole wide world.'

'What can I do then?' he asked.

'Just don't stand in our way.'

'Are you going to marry him, Kieran I mean?'

'We've already started making plans.'

'What, without asking me?'

'What's the point in asking? You've already made crystal clear what your answer'd be. Now, if you'll excuse me, I'm tired and I want to go to sleep.'

Lilly closed her book, placed it on her bedside table and turned out the light, leaving her father to find the door in the dark.

As he closed the door behind him, he whispered, 'I love you Petal.'

Lilly did not reply.

As Alan Henderson changed into his pyjamas in his bedroom in the dark, his wife sat up in bed and switched on her bedside light.

'You're going to lose her, you know,' she said. 'Whether you like it or not, she's going to marry that boy, and if you don't give them your blessing, you'll be losing your daughter, and probably any grandchildren that might come along.'

'She's not pregnant, is she?' he asked alarmed.

'Of course not, you silly old fool. I'm just saying that if you lose her now, you might never see her again.'

Despite a restless night's sleep, Alan Henderson woke the following morning in a more cheerful mood. Lilly had already left for her office job, before he had finished showering. He entered the kitchen just as his wife was making a pot of tea.

'Did you speak to Lilly this morning?' he asked.

'Yes,' his wife replied.

'Did she say anything?'

'About what?'

'You know, about last night.'

'No, not much, why?'

'Oh, no reason. What are we having for dinner tonight?'

'I haven't thought that far ahead yet, why?'

'Any chance we could have a roast? I was thinking of asking Kieran to come and have dinner with us.'

Mrs Henderson almost dropped the teapot in her surprise.

'What's with the change of heart?' she asked when she had recovered her composure.

'Well, if my daughter's hell-bent on marrying this young fellow, I want to get to know him a little bit better.'

'There's no doubt about you; you're full of surprises.'

'Better to be surprised now than afterward when it's too late.'

Alan Henderson did not have Kieran's mobile telephone number, so he had to call his daughter to ask her. While initially reluctant to give it to him, he told her that he only wished to speak with him. He promised her that he would be civil, but he did not tell her of his plan to invite him to dinner. He rang his number.

Kieran usually kept his phone on mute when he was at work so that he would not be disturbed. Late in the afternoon, just before he was due to leave the workshop, he checked his phone. He found a number of missed calls, all from the same number, which he did not recognise. He rang back.

'*Henderson.*'

'Hello, someone on this number called me mobile.'

'*Is that you Kieran?*'

'Yeah, who'zis?'

'*It's Alan Henderson … Lilly's father.*'

'Oh, 'ello Mr 'Enderson, what's up? 'As somethin' 'appened to Lilly?'

'*No, she's fine. I'm wondering if you can come for dinner tonight.*'

Kieran was silent.

'*Are you still there Kieran?*'

'Yeah, I'm 'ere. Gee Mr 'Enderson, it's a bit short notice.'

'*Yes, I'm sorry, but I've been trying to call you all day.*'

'I'll 'ave to call me mum to check with 'er first.'

'*That's alright, but call me straight back, okay? And don't tell Lilly, okay?*'

'Okay.'

Kieran was a little apprehensive as he pulled up outside Lilly's home. While he had been here numerous times in the past year to see his girlfriend, he had never visited at the invitation of her father, and he had never been a guest to dinner. He decided not to ride his motorcycle, believing discretion the better part of valour.

Lilly was completely unaware that Kieran was coming to dinner. When she found out that the family was having roast lamb, and that there would be a guest, she naturally thought that it would be a client or a colleague of her father's. So she was surprised when she opened the front door to a clearly nervous Kieran.

'What are you doing here?' she asked.

'I invited Kieran to dinner,' advised her father from behind her. 'Come in, young man.'

Kieran was very unsure of himself in the presence of Lilly's father. While there had never been open hostility between them, it was no secret that he did not approve of his daughter's relationship with him.

Alan Henderson and his wife were consummate hosts. Kieran's unease was evident, so they made small talk to make him feel more comfortable. All the while, Lilly remained close by to give him moral support.

When the meal was cooked, Alan Henderson carved the meat. Kieran was seated opposite Lilly, with Alan opposite his wife. As always, the guest received the choicest cuts. There were baked vegetables, and thick gravy made from the pan juices, to go with the lamb. After everyone had been served, he said grace before starting the questioning.

'What made you decide to become a motorbike mechanic?'

Kieran had a mouthful of food. When he had swallowed most of it, he answered, 'Me dad used ta race motorbikes. I wanted ta folla in 'is footsteps, but me mum put 'er foot down. She said one racer in the fam'ly was enough. So, I did the nex' bes' thing: I became 'is mechanic.'

'What does your father do now?'

''E owns a metal fabrication business in South Tamworth.'

'What's his name?'

'John Traeghier.'

'Really; is that your dad? I've done some work for him. I didn't know he raced motorbikes.'

After the main course, Mrs Henderson had apple pie and ice cream, or ice cream with topping. Everyone chose the apple pie.

When the dessert dishes had been served, the questioning resumed.

'I understand you want to marry my daughter.'

Alan Henderson was nothing if not forthright. Kieran nearly choked on a mouthful of pie.

'Da-a-d!' Lilly cried out in alarm.

'Be quiet Lilly, you'll get your turn. Right now, I'm speaking with Kieran. So, Kieran …'

When he had recovered enough to speak, he said, 'Yeah, I wanna marry Lilly. We love each other very, very much. I can't imagine bein' with anyone else in the whole world.'

'But how are you going to support her on a mechanic's wage?'

'Me wage's pretty good, and besides, I ain't gonna be a mechanic f'rever. We wanna gedda farm.'

Now it was Alan Henderson's turn to choke on his pie. After a moment he replied, 'Life on the land's pretty tough, working seven days a week with no holidays or sick pay.'

A period of silence followed; the two men stared at one another.

Finally, Kieran spoke, ''Ard work never killed no-one; I never expected an easy life.'

'Properties in the New England cost upwards of a million dollars. Where are you going to get that kind of money?'

Lilly could not remain silent any longer. 'We plan to get experience working on properties, then get into managing one, until we've saved enough to buy what we want.'

'The way you're talking, you make it sound so easy,' advised Mrs Henderson.

Kieran interrupted the discussion. 'Ya missin' the point 'ere. *What* we plan to do in the future, or *how* we do it, ain't what's important 'ere Mr and Mrs 'Enderson. What's important is *who* we're gonna be spendin' the future with. I don't care much about anythin' else, just as long as Lilly's a part of that future with me.'

No-one spoke for several minutes as Kieran's statement sank in. He took the opportunity to finish his dessert.

Eventually Alan Henderson spoke. 'As a parent, I only ever wanted what was best for Lilly. But sometimes, my choices for her, and her choices for herself came into conflict. Some things were non-negotiable; like church and schooling. But with other things I gave her the freedom to choose, knowing that, even if she chose poorly, she might learn from the experience. I would've liked to be able to choose her husband, but I've come to realise that that's going a step too far. I think you're right Kieran; you've got an old head on young shoulders. What you do and how you do it isn't as important as who you do it with. If you two love each other as you say you do, then who am I to stand in the way?'

# Chapter 11

# THE MORNING AFTER

Of all the possible outcomes of an evening spent with the Hendersons, Kieran had not anticipated that he and Lilly would have received their blessing to their plans to get married. He did not sleep very well that night, but not because of any concern that he had; he was just so excited. Lilly was the same. When he awoke early the following morning, he had to text her to confirm that it had not just been something he had dreamed.

Kieran's parents had accepted Lilly right from the start, although they were similarly unaware of their son's wedding plans. When he informed them over breakfast, they were as surprised as the Hendersons. John Traeghier could not understand why they could not live together just as two of his sisters had done with their boyfriends.

'Why can't ya just shack up together? Why do ya have ta get married? Ya jus' so young!'

'I'm a Christian now dad; we don't believe in livin' together,' argued Kieran.

'We're all Christians son; but that didn't stop ya sisters.'

Kieran had already heard this argument from his father. He believed there was little point in trying to again explain to him the fine distinction between his father's ideas of what a Christian was and the reality, so he did not even try. At least his mother did not need an explanation, although she also considered he was too young to get married. Of course, being already nearly 23 years of age, he did not need their approval. But they were still his parents and he loved them.

'Why can't you just wait a coupla years,' she asked, 'until your absolutely certain?'

'I'm absolutely certain now,' he countered. 'What's the point in waitin'?'

His father tried another tack, 'Look Kieran, if you just want ta shag the girl, I can understand – she's very pretty – but you don't need to get married ta 'ave sex.'

'John! Don't say that,' cried Mrs Traeghier.

'Well it's true,' he declared.

Kieran stood up from the breakfast table, 'I thought the 'Endersons were bad enough, but at least they event'ally saw reason. You two're worse.'

He stormed out of the kitchen and went to his room. He was already late for work, so he quickly brushed his teeth before he grabbed his riding gear and left the house.

Kieran was a good motorcycle rider, having been taught well by his father, but he was upset, he was tired from a lack of sleep, and his mind was otherwise engaged – a recipe for disaster.

As he was travelling along Crown Street in South Tamworth at the 50 kmh speed limit, approaching the intersection with the New England Highway, a car pulled out in front of him from a side street, having failed to give way. Normally, Kieran would have anticipated the action of the car driver and had his handbrake covered, ready for an emergency stop. But his mind was elsewhere that morning.

Instead of squeezing the brake firmly, as he had been taught, he grabbed a handful, causing the front wheel to lock. The bike went down with Kieran falling heavily on his left shoulder. His helmet, jacket and gloves did what they were designed to, although they all wore the scars of battle. Except for some minor bruising, he survived the crash, which was more than could be said for his Yamaha. The driver of the car did not stop.

Kieran untangled himself from the bike. He righted his machine to assess the damage. The end of the clutch lever had snapped off, both left side indicator lenses were broken, the handlebars were bent, as was the left-hand mirror, and the tank was dented and scratched. But at least the bike was still rideable. Eventually, someone from a nearby house came to his aid.

'Are you okay mate?' asked the stranger.

'Yeah, I think so,' Kieran replied.

'Do ya ant me ta call the ambulance or police?'

'Nah, I'm awright, really. I jus' need ta rest a few minutes.'

Kieran took his phone from his pocket – at least that had survived the crash unscathed. He called the old mechanic. Katie answered.

'*Classic Bike Repairs and Service, Katie speaking.*'

'Hi Katie, it's Kieran.'

'*Hi Kieran, what's up, did you sleep in?*'

'Nah, I jus' come off me bike.'

'*Are you okay? Do you want us to come and get you?*'

'Nah, I'm okay. I think me bike'll start. I'll jus' be a bit late, that's all.'

'*Where are you?*'

'I'm in South Tamworth, near the 'ighway. I'll be on me way as soon as I c'n get the bike started. See ya.'

'*Bye.*'

He hung up and pocketed his phone. After bending the handlebars and mirror to almost their normal positions, he found that he would be able to make do with the shortened clutch lever. There was nothing he could do about the indicators, but at least all the corners from there on were right handers.

After flicking the kill-switch and turning the ignition key, he brought the piston up to its compression stroke before pushing down hard with his right foot on the kick starter. His Yamaha started first kick. After checking for traffic, he rode off, arriving at the workshop several minutes later without further incident.

The old mechanic was initially annoyed that Kieran was running late, especially as Michael would not be coming in to work that morning. But his annoyance turned to concern with the phone call. He met Kieran as he pulled up in the laneway.

'Are you okay?'

'Yeah, I think so,' replied Kieran as he parked his bike and took off his gloves, helmet and jacket. 'But I could do with a cuppa.'

As he followed the old mechanic back into the workshop, he quickly surveyed the damage to his gear. His gloves and jacket would live to fight another day, but the whack his helmet received meant it was a write-off.

Although Kieran had insurance to cover him against a third-party claim for any damage his motorcycle may have caused to another vehicle in a collision, he was unable to claim for the damage to his bike or his riding gear. Even if he had been able to identify the driver of the other car, he would probably have had difficulty proving who was at fault. And being under 25 years of age, comprehensive insurance cover was out of the question, so even a minor crash could turn out to be a costly exercise.

'Me ol' man won't be impressed when 'e sees the damage to me bike,' advised Kieran.

'I'm sure he'll be relieved that you're alright,' countered Katie.

'What happened?' asked the old mechanic.

Kieran gave a brief outline of the crash, before saying, 'It was me own fault really. Me mind was on other things, 'stead of on what I was doin'.'

'What were you thinking about?' asked Katie.

Kieran suddenly went shy. 'Um, ah, Lilly 'n me are gettin' married.'

Katie gave a squeal of delight. She jumped from her chair and hugged Kieran and gave him a peck on the cheek. 'I'm so happy for you, but …'

The old mechanic finished the question, 'What about Lilly's old man?'

Kieran then related the details of the invitation to the Henderson's place, and of the discussions over dinner. 'At the end, both Mr and Mrs 'Enderson gave us their blessin'. I could 'ardly b'lieve it meself, so I 'ad to tex' Lilly th'smornin' to make sure it wasn' jus' a dream.'

'Is that what was on your mind when you had the crash?' asked the old mechanic.

'That was only 'alf of it. I tol' me parents th'smornin'; they don' wan' us ta get married. Mum wants me to wait; dad said we should jus' live t'gether. 'E doesn' un'erstand that we can't do that.'

'So, what are you gonna do?' asked Katie.

'Me oldies'll eventually come 'round,' Kieran replied with a smile, 'they always do. An' besides, me ol' man'll be so upset about me Yammie, 'e'll 'ave f'gotten all about the weddin'.'

'Speaking of forgetting,' added the old mechanic, 'we're forgetting we've got work to do. Are you alright to work Kieran? There're only the two of us today, so we're gonna be busier than a one-armed paper hanger.'

Katie left the two men to clean up their cups.

'Oh, I forgot, 'ow's Mike?' asked Kieran.

'He's alright,' called Katie from her office. 'He saw a doctor yesterday afternoon. He said there was nothing broken, but he's nursing a pretty good bruise.'

The two mechanics worked well together. The old mechanic never ceased to be impressed by the younger man's skills, knowledge and understanding of all things to do with classic British motorcycles. Whether a bike was a single, twin or triple cylinder, two-stroke or four, side-valve, overhead valve or overhead camshaft, Kieran was comfortable working on it. Even when faced with something new, he only had to be shown once, and he was an instant expert.

By the mid-morning break, both men had completed two customer bikes each. But the delayed effects of his earlier crash were starting to be felt. As the two men took a break for smoko, Kieran's head and shoulder were beginning to ache.

''Ave we got any pain killers?' he asked Katie.

'Do you have a headache?'

'Yeah, I feel like I've got the mother o' all 'angovers, an' me shoulder's startin' ta stiffen up.'

'I think you should probably go an' see a doctor,' suggested the old mechanic.

'Nah, I'll be okay with some 'eadache tablets,' said Kieran.

'You were on your way to work when you had the accident,' advised Katie, 'so it'll be covered by Worker's Comp. You won't have to pay for it.'

'Nah, 'onestly, I'll be okay,' repeated Kieran, 'jus' gimme some tablets please.'

The old mechanic kept his eye on Kieran for the remainder of the day. While he said he felt okay, he could tell that the younger man was suffering a degree of discomfort with his shoulder. At least he seemed prepared to suffer in relative silence.

'I don't think you should be ridin' your motorbike home this arvo,' suggested the old mechanic at the end of the day. 'We can load your Yammie onto the back of the truck and give you both a ride home.'

'But …'

'I'm not asking Kieran.'

The two men were quiet for the short journey back to Kieran's place. As they pulled up outside the driveway, Kieran spoke, 'I'm sorry ta put you ta all this trouble George.'

'Kieran, it's no trouble. And if you're still feeling unwell in the morning, please call the workshop, and then go see a doctor. You'll probably be stiff 'n sore anyway, but if you can't come in to work, let me know.'

'Yeah, I will.'

As Kieran had expected, his mother was more worried for her son's health and safety, while his father's concern was for the bike. Nothing more was said of the wedding plans.

Earlier in the day, Katie had contacted Lilly and told her about the accident while at the same time congratulating her on their engagement. Lilly called in to see Kieran on her way home from her office job. His mother answered the knock to the door.

'Hello Lilly dear,' said Kieran's mother.

'Hello Mrs Traeghier, is Kieran home?'

'Yes, he's in his bedroom.'

Lilly followed Mrs Traeghier through the house to Kieran's room. In all the time that they had been going out together, she had only ever been in the living areas of his house; she had yet to see where Kieran slept.

She knocked softly at his door. There was no answer. She called his name. Still there was no answer. A young single woman entering a man's bedroom was normally forbidden for devout Christians, but she felt compelled to enter. Her heart was pounding; she felt a tingle of excitement as she turned the door handle.

It took some moments for Lilly's eyes to adjust to the gloom of the bedroom. Her fiancée was sleeping bare-chested on top of the bed clothes, his hands behind his head. She made her way silently to his bedside and sat on the edge. His musky odour was intoxicating. She bent down and kissed him full on the lips. Immediately he responded; his eyes and mouth opened and his arms quickly enveloped her upper body.

They kissed long and slowly. He could feel her breasts straining on the buttons of her blouse against his chest. They were so close, he wanted to touch them, caress them, squeeze them, but he knew he could not. For those few moments he forgot the ache in his shoulder.

At length, Lilly pulled away from his grasp. 'We can't,' she said, breathless, 'we have to wait.'

'Yeah!' was all he could think to say.

When she recovered her breath she asked, 'How're you feeling?'

'Much better now, thanks ta you. I didn' realise you 'ad the gift o' 'ealin',' he said with a smile.

'I've got lots of gifts that you didn't realise I had;' she replied evenly, 'but you'll just have to wait 'til we're married before you can open them.'

# Chapter 12

## VARIATIONS ON A THEME

Both younger mechanics made it into work the following morning, although they each had to catch a lift to do so. Michael arrived with Katie, while Kieran hitched a lift from his father. Michael still walked with a slight limp, but at least he was now able to ride his Norton – he would ride it home. Kieran's shoulder was feeling much better after a good night's sleep and, following the visit from Lilly, his headache had disappeared. Even though Kieran was also able to ride, he was now without a serviceable helmet, not to mention a serviceable bike of his own.

The three mechanics and Katie came together for their usual early morning cuppa. While the three men made their own beverages, Katie decided to abstain – the aroma of coffee being a constant threat to bring on another bout of morning sickness. Instead, she preferred to stick to plain old chilled tap water from the refrigerator.

Once the four of them were settled, the old mechanic asked Katie, 'Are you entitled to take Maternity Leave from your office job in Tamworth?'

'Our Award doesn't include Paid Maternity Leave,' she replied, 'but I think I can still take all my accrued leave, as well as Leave Without Pay of up to 12 months. But since I started working Part-Time, I'm not sure what I'm entitled to.'

'Can you take advantage of the Government's new Paid Maternity Leave Scheme?' asked Michael.

'Yeah, I think so, but I think you only get paid for 18 weeks at the Minimum Wage. Still, I suppose that's better than nothing.'

'It used to be that, unless you worked for the Government, you weren't entitled to anything,' advised the old mechanic.

Katie turned to Kieran, 'Have you set a date for the wedding yet?'

'Nah, not yet. If I 'ad my way, we'd duck down to the Registry Office at lunch time, but Lilly wants a big church weddin' with all the trimmin's,' Kieran replied.

'I'd have thought that now you're a Christian, you'd have wanted a church wedding,' Katie continued. 'You know, to get God's blessing and all.'

'Churches are jus' buildin's; God c'n still bless a marriage no matter where it takes place.'

'That'd be ironic,' interjected Michael. 'Me and Katie are non-believers, and we get married in a church; you and Lilly *are* believers, and you don't.'

'I didn' say we weren't getting' married in a church, jus' that I wouldn't care if we did.'

'Speaking of caring, we've got some bikes to take care of,' interrupted the old mechanic. 'Who's doin' what Mike?'

'We've had a rush of two-stroke twins come in the workshop: a couple of tiddlers and the weirdest looking classic bike I've ever seen, a Scott Flying Squirrel. There's also an Ariel Red Hunter, a Norton Model 50, a Trumpy TR5 and a BSA M21.'

'What's wrong with the two smokes?' asked the old mechanic.

'The owner of the Greeves Sports told me that one of the plugs keeps oilin' up, so it's running rich on one cylinder,' related Michael, 'and the James' owner says his Superswift seized up when he went for a ride on Sunday. The Scott needs new brake shoes.'

'I'll do the pair o' two-stroke twins,' volunteered Kieran with a grin. 'I love workin' on two-smokes.'

Both the Greeves Sports and the James Superswift used a proprietary two-stroke engine produced by the Villiers Engineering Company of Villiers Street, Wolverhampton. In both cases, they were 250cc twins. Until the 1960s, Villiers manufactured a range of single and twin two-stroke engines spanning 98cc to 325cc for a number of motorcycle manufacturers; among them Excelsior, Francis-Barnett, Greeves, James and Panther, as well as many smaller makes.

'I love workin' on 'em too,' advised the old mechanic, 'so I'll do the Scott.'

The Scott Flying Squirrel could trace its origins back to the 1920s when production began. In the immediate post war years, the company produced motorcycles featuring twin cylinder, two-stroke water-cooled motors. But the bikes were expensive and very heavy. When the company went into liquidation in the early 1950s production ceased only to restart when enthusiast Matt Holder began production in Birmingham in 1956. The Birmingham Scotts featured a capacity of 596cc, a duplex frame, telescopic front forks and swinging arm rear suspension. The model in the workshop was one of these later models.

'Hey, I thought I was the one to divvy out the jobs,' cried Michael.

'Okay,' conceded the old mechanic, with a look of disappointment, 'you're the boss.'

Michael smiled saying, 'Um, Kieran, you can start on the two two-stroke twins and George, you can start on the Flying Squirrel. Having said that, I'm not sure we have spares for any of them.'

'The Villiers engines won't be a problem, but the Scott might be; I'll check.'

As the old mechanic expected, there were no spares in the storeroom made specifically for the Scott Flying Squirrel. However, items like cables, chains, hand controls, and shoes for the drum brakes, were generic items which, with some minor modifications, could be adapted to fit.

By mid-morning, Kieran had adjusted the jetting in the carburettor of the Greeves so that it ran without oiling the sparkplug and he had stripped the top end of the James' motor and replaced one of the pistons. The barrels appeared to be undamaged, so he left them alone. He also found that one cylinder was running hot, which was the likely cause of the seizure – an incorrect spark plug was suspected of being the culprit. While the Villiers twin engines were a step up in complexity compared to the humble BSA Bantam two-stroke single, they were still very simple to work on compared with a four-stroke single cylinder motor like the one in the Ariel Red Hunter or the BSA M21.

Once the old mechanic had replaced the worn brake shoes on the Scott, and Michael had completed servicing the Ariel, the three mechanics and Katie came together for smoko.

As they waited for the jug to boil, Kieran asked the question that had been at the back of his mind since he started, 'Why do we only look after ol' Pommie bikes? Why don' we fix up Jap bikes like me Yammie?'

'Ah Kieran, do you want the long answer or the short answer?' asked the old mechanic.

Kieran shrugged his shoulders, 'I don' care. 'Ow long's the long answer?'

'Probably longer than we've got. I tell you what, I'll give you a summary of the long answer,' he replied with a smile.

'When my old man first started up the business, there were very few Japanese motorcycles. All the big-name bikes in the country came from Britain, with a few from America, Germany and Italy thrown in. The business was built on servicing and repairing what have become classic British motorcycles. And the thing that keeps our business going now is the availability of spare parts. Since the demise of the British motorcycle, and the resurgence of what are now classic bikes, a new industry emerged producing spare parts to keep them on the road. While the classic Japanese bikes may appear to be just variations on a theme, there isn't the same level of spares backup to make it viable to support them.'

'But I can still get spares for me Yammie,' countered Kieran.

'Yes granted, but that's because the SR400/500s 've been in production pretty much unchanged since the 1970s, and it's been one of their more enduring models. But generally, the Japanese have short model runs and quick turn-arounds. Look how many versions they've had over the years of Suzuki's GSXR750. If you had one of the first models, you'd have almost no hope of finding spare parts for it. Now compare that to my Norton Dominator; I could almost buy enough spares to build one from scratch if I wanted to, and had enough money.'

'But the Norton Dommie changed over the life of the model,' argued Kieran.

'True, but many of the parts remained unchanged. And even when items were improved, they could often be retrofitted into earlier models of the same bike.'

'What if we could look after selected classic Jap models; things like Honda CB750s and Kawasaki W650s?' suggested Michael hopefully. 'That would also help cushion the winter downturn.'

'Yeah, it might,' replied the old mechanic. 'But there're a coupla problems. First is we'd need to invest in a whole workshop full of new tools. All the Japanese, as well as the Europeans use metric, while the British are all imperial.'

'I know whacha mean,' interrupted Kieran. 'We 'ad ta get all new imperial spanners 'n stuff when we started restorin' me Bonnie.'

'Oh, how's the restoration going?' asked the old mechanic.

'Yeah, good. We've jus' about finished the motor. On the weekend, I'm gonna show dad 'ow ta relace the wheels.'

'Good for you. Do you wanna borrow the Mercer gauges?'

'That'd be great if we could.'

'You said there were a couple of problems,' interjected Michael, impatiently, 'you only mentioned one.'

'Well, the second, and even greater problem, is how we inform the customer that we're discriminating between the different types of classic Japanese motorcycles. At the moment, we don't differentiate between the different types of classic British bikes. If you've got a Pommie classic, we'll look after it. But for the average punter, a classic Jap bike is, as I said earlier, just a variation on a theme. So, it's all or it's nothing.'

Michael responded with a glum expression on his face.

'Don't worry Mike,' asserted the old mechanic, as he rose from his seat to resume work, 'we've still got plenty here to keep us busy for now.'

Yeah, for now, thought Michael, but what about later?

With Kieran unable to ride due to the lack of a serviceable helmet, the old mechanic took on the duties of test riding all of the machines. After he returned from riding all three two-stroke engined motorcycles, he resumed the restoration of the Vincent Comet. Kieran started on the Norton 350, while Michael started on the BSA 600cc M21 single.

The Norton Model 50 was a rare machine to find intact, especially the later models featuring the famed featherbed frame, like the one in the workshop. A large proportion of these motorcycles had been modified at some stage in their life; the 350cc motor being discarded in favour of a larger capacity donor engine to make a café racer. The motor most often used was either a 650cc or 750cc Triumph Bonneville; the resultant motorcycle being referred to as a Triton. But the well-heeled or well-connected motorcyclist, who had access to the Vincent 998cc V-twin motor, used it to create the much coveted Norvin.

The Model 50 in the workshop featured the "slimline" featherbed frame. It was one of the last of that model to emerge from the Norton factory having been manufactured in 1963, the year production ceased. The owner had purchased the motorcycle already restored, but the motor was still being run-in. The valve tappets and the timing needed adjustment, and the engine oil, as well as the oil in the gearbox needed replacement.

As Michael started working on the BSA, he was reminded of the BSA M33 that he had modified the previous year. In common with that machine, the M21 had a plunger frame. The plunger frame appeared in the late 1940s and, though an improvement on the old rigid set-up, was inferior to the later swinging arm that is still employed today. The disadvantages of the plunger suspension over the swingarm included: wheel travel that was limited; the wheel was not stable and could move out of the required vertical axis; and it was more expensive to produce and maintain.

While he worked, Michael called to the old mechanic, 'Hey George, whatever happened to old Jim Fredericks, the guy who owned the Beeza M33 that we modified?'

'You mean you modified.'

'Yeah, him.'

'He died from a stroke late last year; I think you an' Katie'd just got married. You were away on your honeymoon when funeral was on.'

'Poor guy. Did you ever hear what happened to his bike?'

'No, but I'm guessing his daughter might've inherited it. If you remember, she rode the bike here to the workshop and you gave her a lift home on your bike.'

'Yeah, I remember. What was her name again?'

'Stephanie ... Stephanie O'Brien.'

'Oh, that's right.'

Katie emerged from her office, catching the tail end of the conversation, 'Who's Stephanie O'Brien?'

'She was just the daughter of a guy we did some work for,' replied Michael.

'What happened to her?'

'Nothing that we know of, but her old man died late last year.' Turning back to the old mechanic, Michael continued, 'I hope the owner of this bike doesn't hear that we modified Jim's old machine; I'd hate him to get any ideas.'

'Yeah, we've already had enough variations on a theme for one day.'

The two mechanics laughed.

# Chapter 13

# RIDING WITH MATES

The week had been fairly busy, with plenty of classic motorcycles passing through the workshop for maintenance, repairs or a service. Kieran had ordered a new helmet from the Helmet Warehouse, and it had arrived via overnight courier, so he was once again able to test ride the machines that he had worked on. With new indicator lenses, a left-hand mirror, and a pair of ace-bars to replace the old bent clip-ons, he was mobile once more. He and Michael arrived for work together on the Friday morning.

'I missed ridin' to work with you,' advised Kieran when both men had parked their bikes and removed their helmets.

'How's the new lid,' asked Michael.

'It's t'rrific: light, quiet and comf'table – what more could ya want?'

'Cheap?' suggested Michael.

Kieran laughed. 'Three outa four ain't bad.'

'What's not bad?' asked the old mechanic who caught the tail-end of the conversation.

'My new helmet,' answered Kieran.

Kieran handed his new helmet to the old mechanic.

'Gee it's light; what's it made of?'

'Carbon-fibre composite,' reported Kieran.

'Expensive?'

'Of course, but as me ol' man sez, "what price do ya put on safety?" And besides, 'e paid for it, said it was an early birthd'y present.'

'I wish my old man'd buy me birthday presents like that,' lamented Michael enviously.

'Have you heard from your father since he left?' asked the old mechanic.

'I get the odd birthday and Christmas card from him, but he never says anything, and he never gives a forwarding address.'

'Does 'e know you're married now?' asked Kieran.

'Probably not, but I couldn't care less even if he does.'

'I'd hate for my ol' man to leave me mum.'

'Depends how bad things are at home. Sometimes it's the lesser of two evils.' Just when the conversation was threatening to become a touch gloomy, Michael announced, 'Anyway, enough of this, we've got work to do.'

As the two younger mechanics commenced working on the various customer bikes, the old mechanic resumed his restoration of the Vincent Comet. While the engine in the Comet was quite literally half that of a Vincent Black Shadow's 998cc V-twin, all of the cycle parts were pretty much the same as that of the larger engined motorcycle. This meant that the power-to-weight ration of the Comet was about half that of its bigger brother. Notwithstanding, the Comet was no slouch when it came to performance, and could compete favourably against any other machine in its class.

Being a single cylinder motor, there was half of everything compared to the V-twin: half the pistons, half the rings, the valves, valve-springs, pushrods, tappets, heads, barrels, carburettors, and so on. Accordingly, it was a much simpler task reassembling everything. Once he had ascertained that the work previously completed by the late former owner had been done correctly, the old mechanic proceeded apace to finish the job.

By the mid-morning break, he had completed the motor, and by lunch time he had serviced the carburettor and bolted it onto the inlet side of the cylinder head. With the other two still busy servicing and repairing customer bikes, the old mechanic took it upon himself to collect the lunches from the sandwich bar.

As he was returning from the shop, he noticed a motorcycle rider pass him on the opposite side of the road, slow down, pull over and then turn around, pulling up beside the old mechanic. It was not until the rider opened his visor and spoke that the old mechanic realised it was Jim Browning.

'Hello George, fancy meetin' you here.'

'G'day Jim; I live here. My workshop's just around the corner. D'ya wanna come and see what I do for a crust?'

'Yeah, I'd love to.' Jim then noticed the sandwiches. 'Is it lunchtime?'

'Yeah, it's nearly midday; you can get something at the shop and come an' eat with us if you want?'

'Okay, but don't wait for me. Just tell me where your workshop is.'

'Up the road, take the first right, there's a laneway behind the houses, turn right again. We're about a hundred metres up the lane.'

'Sure, I'll be there as soon as I can.'

'I'll have the jug boiling for a cuppa.'

'Terrific, I'll have coffee thanks, NATO Standard.'

The old mechanic had just finished stirring Jim's cup of coffee when he heard the sound of his Triumph Bonneville T100 coming down the laneway. He met him as he removed his helmet.

'Welcome to my humble abode,' announced the old mechanic.

'So, is this where you make a silk purse out of a sow's ear?' teased Jim smiling.

'No, we don't have any Harley's here,' replied the old mechanic evenly. 'All the bikes are British, with the exception of Kieran's.'

'Touché, I probably deserved that.'

The old mechanic did not reply, but nodded in agreement. Jim followed him into the workshop, to the area where the two younger mechanics were already tucking into their sandwiches. The old mechanic introduced him.

'You know Mike. This is Kieran.'

Michael nodded while Kieran shook Jim's hand, but said nothing as his mouth was full. The two older men sat down and started eating.

When they were settled, the old mechanic asked, 'So what brings you here?'

'Actually,' replied Jim, 'I was just going for a ride when I recognised you walking toward me up the street. I've been curious to know where Mike worked since he did that job for me, so it was fortuitous that I ran into you.'

'Where would you have gone if you hadn't seen me?'

'Oh, nowhere in particular. You know what they say, "the ride *is* the destination".'

'I enjoyed the ride last Saturday,' said the old mechanic. 'It seems such a long time ago now. So much has happened this week.'

'Do you usually go for a ride on the weekend?'

'When I get the chance. I'm usually busy Saturdays with domestics, so Sund'y's my usual time. But last Sunday I had commitments, so I stole some time Saturd'y arvo, which is when I met you at Quirindi.'

'Do ya feel like goin' for a ride this Sund'y?' asked Jim.

The old mechanic felt trapped. Although he had ridden with Jim most of the journey home from Quirindi, they were not riding together as such. It would be a completely different prospect going for a ride *with* someone. When he rode by himself, he was in control; he set the pace, the route, the rest stops, and the refuelling stops. But when he rode with someone else, especially if he was not familiar with the other person's riding style, he felt he would no longer have that control.

Jim sensed his unease. 'You can take the lead, if ya like.'

'Is there anywhere you'd like to go?'

'No, not really. Why don't you surprise me?'

'Alright, I'll drop by your place at 10:00 am sharp Sunday morning.'

'I'll be ready.'

Despite his misgivings, the old mechanic awoke early Sunday morning feeling excited at the prospect of a day's riding. Preparing to ride a classic British motorcycle like the Norton Dominator was not like readying a more modern machine. Whereas the only things needed for a late model motorbike was to adjust and lubricate the chain, refuel and check the tyre pressures, much more was required for a classic machine. Besides all these, the old mechanic topped up the oil, lubricated and adjusted the throttle, brake and clutch cables, checked the clutch adjustment, adjusted the tappets, and ran a spanner over every nut and a screwdriver over every screw to ensure that they were all tight so that nothing would fall off. Only when he had completed everything was the bike ready to ride.

The old mechanic was a traditionalist when it came to riding apparel. While most riders wore either leathers or weather-proof fabric jackets and pants, he preferred his old

Belstaff wax-cotton jacket and denim jeans. And while most wore full-face helmets, he preferred an open-face with aviator type goggles. At least he had good quality boots and gloves.

He arrived at the Banjo Creek address just before the appointed hour. Jim was already dressed and was wheeling his Bonneville out of his garage. Michael heard the sound of his father-in-law's Norton and opened the door of his Unit. While he would have loved to join them for the ride, Katie had already made other plans for the morning that had nothing to do with motorcycles. Maybe next time, he thought as he waved the two men off.

The Sunday morning traffic was relatively light, with only the occasional car heading for church, or the netball-mum driving the SUV with a load of kids heading to a game. Once out of the built-up area, and the more restrictive speed zones, the old mechanic upped the pace. At Nemingha, he turned right off the Oxley Highway onto the road to Nundle, but instead of going through the roundabout, he turned left and took the Back Kootingal Road which loosely follows the Cockburn River. At Kootingal, he turned right on the road that leads to Limbri which continues to follow the river. This road was narrow, but well sealed and, with little traffic, the two men were enjoying the ride.

At Limbri, the road continues on to Weabonga, now following Swamp Oak Creek. Except for the tiny settlement of Weabonga, with nothing more than a dozen houses, there was little sign of civilisation. They had passed only three vehicles, two dogs, a couple of stray sheep and one cow. They had seen no shops, and certainly nowhere to refuel. Jim kept doggedly behind the old mechanic, sometimes within 20 metres, but at other times more than 250 metres, but he seemed to be enjoying himself as much as the old mechanic was.

After Weabonga, they continued on until the intersection with Post Office Street. While called a street, it seemed little more than a track to the two riders. The street ended at Ogunbil, quite literally a one house hamlet. Turning right into Ogunbil Road which followed Dungowan Creek, Jim was beginning to wonder when they might see signs of humanity. Other than the few cattle and sheep, the only other terrestrial creatures they saw was a sole eastern grey kangaroo resting under a gumtree in a paddock, an echidna, and five red belly black snakes. Had they stopped, they would have heard, if not seen, the screeching flocks of corellas and galahs, the plaintive cries of large black crows and the maniacal laugh of the occasional kookaburra.

Ogunbil Road ends at the intersection with the road to Nundle. After slowing for the tiny village of Woolomin, the road follows the Peel River to Chaffey Dam. After skirting the large lake caused by damming the river, the road becomes the River Road which wends its way into Nundle. By the time the two men slowed for this large sleepy village, they were in desperate need of a drink and some food, a toilet stop and for their nether-regions, relief from numb-bum syndrome. Their bikes were also in desperate need of fuel.

There was only one service station-cum-garage in Nundle, and it was usually closed on Sundays. However, the Country Café next door was owned by the same family, and the owner was happy to sell the pair enough fuel to get them on their way, together with a works burger and a cold soft drink. Jim had harboured a secret desire to quench his thirst with an ice-cold beer, but the village pub did not sell petrol, so he had to be satisfied with the offerings from the café.

'Didja like that road Jim?' asked the old mechanic while they were refuelling.

Jim was busy massaging his backside, trying to get the blood circulating and some feeling returned. 'Absolutely! Ya know I've lived in Tamworth me whole life and I've never been on some of them roads. How d'ja find 'em?'

'When you're in the business of fixin' old bikes, sometimes you need a nice quiet back-road to give 'em a good fang. I've been ridin' these roads my whole workin' life.'

'Ya must like bein' a motorbike mechanic.'

'Yeah, other than road testin' virgins for the Shah of Persia, I can't think of a job I'd rather be doin'.'

Jim laughed; he had never heard that comparison before. And every time he thought of the saying on the way home, he laughed again.

With full tanks and bellies, the two men left Nundle and, instead of heading back to Tamworth, they continued on Crawney Road toward Timor. The road became very narrow and windy as it made its way down the escarpment from the New England Plateau to the floor of the Hunter Valley. Some way along, it followed the Isis River and then Timor Creek. At Timor, they turned right onto Timor Road toward the New England Highway. Entering the highway just to the northwest of Blandford, they rode the short distance to Murrurundi.

In the township of Murrurundi there were several places to refuel, so they could afford to be choosey. After another drink and a rest stop, they rode the ten kilometres to Chilcotts Creek Road where they turned off the highway for the return trip and home. After leading all of the way so far, the old mechanic signalled for Jim to overtake him. At Woodton Road Jim slowed, but seeing that Chilcotts Creek Road was unsealed beyond the intersection, he turned left. When they came to the highway again, he was unsure whether to turn right or left. Looking in his mirrors, he saw the old mechanic pointing left. Less than a kilometre down the highway is Hamiltons Road where they turned right. Hamiltons Road led to Wallabadah Road where, turning left, Jim was in familiar territory. From Quirindi, there were a number of options for the route home, but Jim chose the way he was most familiar with, the road through Werris Creek, Currabubula and Duri.

As he approached his home, the old mechanic tooted his horn and waved while Jim continued on to Banjo Creek. It had been a long time since he had last been out riding with a mate, but he hoped it would not be as long until the next time.

# Chapter 14

# AN OBLIGATION FULFILLED

The restoration of the Vincent Comet was progressing well. Over the following weeks, and in between helping the two younger men service, repair and otherwise maintain all manner of classic British motorcycles, the old mechanic relaced the wheels with new stainless-steel spokes, replaced the tyres, sent the seat to be recovered, and the fuel tank to be repainted.

While the late previous owner had already repainted the tank, the old mechanic was dissatisfied with the finish, believing that the old man had probably painted it himself. The tank had a slight orange-peel finish and the pin-striping was poorly applied, while the tank lacked a coat of clear lacquer to keep transfers from wearing off. A short trip to his spray painter mate in South Tamworth had the tank looking better than new in a little over a fortnight.

Once he had the seat and tank returned and installed, the old mechanic was ready to get the old Vincent back on the road. After fitting a new fully-charged 6-volt battery, filling the oil tank with Penrite Enduro premium mineral oil and filling the newly finished fuel tank with 95 octane fuel, he was ready to start the motor.

The Vincent Comet has a decompression lever that allows easier starting of the engine. When the lever is employed, as the name suggests, the compression of the air in the cylinder is reduced, thereby allowing the kick-starter to more easily spin the motor. The trick is to release the lever at the same time that the engine sparks into life.

The old mechanic wheeled the Comet out of the workshop and into the laneway, placing it on the centre-stand. After turning on the fuel and priming the carburettor, he turned the decompression lever, straddled the bike and brought the cylinder to the top of its compression stroke. By this time, he had an audience; Katie, Michael and Kieran stopped their work and left the workshop to watch.

On more modern motorcycles, the old mechanic would also have turned on the ignition, but on many old classic machines, such as the Vincent Comet, there was no ignition switch, or key for that matter. He twisted the accelerator to about a quarter turn and pushed down hard with his right leg on the kick-starter. It coughed, but did not start. He repeated the process and pushed down hard on the kick-starter again. It coughed again, but he released the decompression lever too early and the kick start lever slipped off his boot and caught him on the back of his leg. He dismounted, massaging his right calf muscle.

'D'ya want me to 'ave a go?' asked Kieran.

'Okay, but be careful; it'll kick like a mule with a bad temper if ya don't watch yaself.'

Kieran smiled; he had not heard that saying before. 'Yeah, I will.'

While the younger man had never tried to start a Vincent Comet before, he was very experienced in starting 500cc single cylinder motorcycles, with or without a decompression lever. And although he was lighter than the old mechanic, he was fitter and had quicker reflexes. On his second attempt at kick starting, the motor coughed into life. After a few minutes warming the engine, it settled into an even idle, with the exhaust rumbling.

'It started easier than I expected,' remarked Michael. 'I half expected we'd have the same trouble we had with the Black Shadow.'

'I wasn't expecting any trouble,' replied the old mechanic. 'If you remember, the Shadow wasn't standard, where this one's exactly as it was when it first emerged from the factory 65 years ago.'

'That makes it the same age as you, Dad,' teased Katie.

'Yeah, thanks for reminding me, Sweetheart. But I wouldn't mind bein' the same as I was when I first emerged from the factory.'

'Not me,' countered Kieran, 'I love being who I am now. I'd hate to go back ta bein' a baby again.'

'Yeah, on reflection, goin' back 65 years might be a bit much, but bein' 30- or 40-years younger'd be nice.'

'I'm with Kieran,' insisted Michael, 'I wouldn't want to be anything other than I am now. And besides, if you lose the years, you also lose the experiences, and that's what life's all about.'

'You're becoming all philosophical now,' replied the old mechanic. 'Anyway, enough of all this talk; I'm taking the Comet for a test ride.'

When the old mechanic returned, Katie had left the workshop to collect the sandwiches for lunch. Michael met him as he dismounted from the Comet.

'How was it?'

'It's okay,' replied the old mechanic.

'Okay? Is that all?' Michael was dismayed.

'Yeah, I've never been a big fan of the Vincent chassis. And while the motor's strong, and will only get better as it's run in, I reckon the handling's compromised by the Girdraulic forks. While the engine in your Norton mightn't be as powerful as the Comet's, its featherbed frame wins hands down.'

'But that won't stop it from selling will it?'

'Of course not; people buy a Vincent because it's a Vincent, not because of the handling.'

'So, when're you putting it on the market?'

'Once I get it registered, and fulfil my obligation to the lady who sold it to me, it can go on eBay.'

Katie's return from the sandwich shop signalled that it was time for lunch, so the conversation was cut short while the old mechanic parked the Vincent and returned his riding gear to the storeroom.

When everyone was seated and tucking into their lunches, Michael enquired, 'So what's your obligation to the lady who sold you the Vincent?'

'She made me promise that, when I'd finished the restoration, I'd show it to her husband.'

'But he's dead, isn't he?' Michael was incredulous.

'Yeah,' replied the old mechanic deadpan.

'You're not serious, are you?'

'Of course I'm serious.'

'You're going to ride four hours up to Guyra and back, just to show the bike to someone who's already dead; that's crazy!' asserted Michael.

'Look Mike, crazy it may be, but the only reason I got this Vincent for the price I paid for it, was because I agreed to show the finished article to the lady's late husband. That four hour ride probably saved us five thousand bucks. So you tell me, what's better, spending ten grand for a ten grand bike or spending five for a ten grand bike? I'm happy to be labelled crazy if that saves us five grand. For five grand, I'd even ride naked to Guyra and back. And remember, we'll probably be able to sell the bike for 25 grand or more, meaning we can make upwards of $15,000 profit. Who cares if the old man's dead, just as long as it makes his widow happy? And remember, I made a promise to her, and I'm not about to renege on it.'

Michael digested the information as he finished his sandwiches. At last he said, 'For five grand, I'd ride naked to Guyra and back myself.'

'I wouldn't,' declared Kieran, 'I'd be too embarrassed.'

'Same here. I wouldn't do a Lady Godiva act for anyone.' Katie was nodding her head as she spoke. 'So Dad, when're going?'

'I've still gotta get the bike registered, then I'll give her a call to arrange a time to visit. She'll probably want to come along to make sure it happens.'

'Do you know where the old guy's buried?' asked Michael.

'No. I guess I'll find that out when I get to Guyra.'

The old mechanic had little trouble getting the Vincent Comet registered. Having completed the process twice previously in the last few years, the people at the Motor Registry Office knew him well and he was familiar with their procedures. With new numberplates fitted to the motorcycle, he dialled the old lady's number.

'*Hello.*'

'Oh, hello, um, is Mrs Spencer there?'

'*No, she isn't available at the moment. Would you like to leave a message?*'

'Yes, it's George Edwards from Classic Bike Repairs and Service ...'

'*Hello Mr Edwards, mum said you might call. I'm Maggie Dawes, Joan Spencer's daughter. Mum's not very well at the moment; she's in the hospital undergoing tests.*'

'I'm sorry to hear that. Did she tell you why I'd call?'

'Yes, I'm under strict instructions to show you where dad's burial plot is.'

'Did she tell you why?'

'*Oh yes. Have you finished restoring dad's old bike?*'

'Yep, it's all finished and registered, ready for many more years of service.'

'*When were you planning to come up?*'

'I was thinking about this Sunday, if that's convenient?'

'*Yes, that's fine. What time do you think you'll be here?*'

'If I leave home at ten, I should be there about midday.'

'*Good. I'll meet you at the cemetery.*'

'Okay then, I'll see you there. Bye.'

'*Bye.*'

The old mechanic hung up the telephone. When he was dealing with the old lady, he was happy to entertain her eccentricities, but now that her daughter was involved, he felt a little awkward, but he felt obligated to fulfil his promise.

It was already lunchtime and Michael had his sandwiches ready for him. The jug had boiled and the two younger men were each preparing their beverages. The old mechanic joined them.

'You ridin' the Vincent up to Guyra?' asked Kieran in between gulps of coffee.

'I was thinkin' about it, but it's a fair hike on an old classic like the Comet. So no, I'll probably throw it on the back of the truck and drive up. And besides, I wanna keep the paint as pristine as possible with no stone chips; I can't do that if I ride it.'

'You going up the highway?' asked Michael.

'The other options take twice the time, and aren't that much more interestin' anyway. Now, if I was going up there for pleasure, I'd take the long way 'round. But for the quick trip there and back, the New England's the way to go.'

"'Opefully this time, there won't be any thunderstorms and truck crashes,' quipped Kieran.

'We can only hope Kieran,' replied the old mechanic, 'we can only hope.'

Sunday dawned fine and sunny, with a cool south-westerly breeze blowing. While it would have been a great day to ride the bike, the old mechanic stuck to his plan. On the Friday afternoon, he had the two younger mechanics help him load the truck, so all he had to do on the day was drive.

There was little traffic on the highway going north, except around Armidale. Most semi-trailers and b-doubles heading from Sydney to Brisbane or back again use the Pacific Highway. Only those heading to or from Melbourne use the New England.

The Guyra Lawn Cemetery is located about five minutes drive south of the township just off the highway. The old mechanic arrived with about ten minutes to spare. As he drove in through the gates, he noticed a number of people who appeared to be visiting graves; some were laying flowers, while others were tidying up around grave sites. There was no car park as such, but he noticed a car parked on the side of the road just ahead of him. When he pulled in behind the car, a woman got out and approached his car. The old mechanic wound down his window.

The woman asked, 'Are you George Edwards?'

'Sure am! Are you Maggie?'

'Yes, and my husband, Stan's in the car. I was wondering whether you'd ride or drive.'

'I wanted to keep the bike in good condition to show your dad. How's your mum?'

'Not very good; she's been transferred to Armidale Hospital. If she ever gets out, it'll be into a nursing home.'

Maggie continued, 'Actually, I feel a little bit embarrassed. I only went along with it to humour mum. I didn't really think you'd call, and I certainly didn't think you'd come.'

'Well, I did promise her that I'd show Jack his pride and joy, so you'd better tell me where he's been laid to rest.'

'It's straight ahead; take the track to the right, his headstone is the last one in the first row.'

'Are you coming?'

'Yeah; I'll follow you. I want to take some photos to show mum, just in case she asks.'

'Ah! Incriminating evidence,' suggested the old mechanic with a smile.

Having brought the restored Vincent Comet to the graveside of Joan Spencer's late husband, the old mechanic parked his truck as close to the headstone as he could. He alighted from the cabin and let down the aluminium sides before climbing up on the tray to remove the tarpaulin concealing the restored motorcycle. Once revealed, he stood back and spoke.

'Um, g'day Jack, um, I hope you can see your old Vincent from where you are. Your dear wife entrusted me to restore it for you. I hope you're happy with the results.'

At that moment, in the distance, the plaintive cry of a crow could be heard. Ark, ark, aaark.

'I think he's happy with the bike,' declared Maggie.

'Yeah, I hope so.'

The old mechanic returned home later that afternoon with a sense of satisfaction that he had fulfilled his obligation.

# Chapter 15

# TRADING CLASSICS

The best time to sell a classic motorcycle is normally at the beginning of the riding season. But in Australia, where the weather permits year-round riding, sellers can often find buyers at almost any time of the year, although in the New England area, the winter months of July and August are typically the time for the ardent enthusiast only.

While the Vincent name frequently evokes a passionate response from many classic British motorcycle aficionados, the old mechanic was past caring about the Vincent Comet he had just restored. In his mind it was nothing particularly special. Rather than being an end in itself, it was merely a means to an end, with the end being to make money.

The old mechanic's skills on the computer had progressed well over the last four years since he had purchased his first laptop, although he was still a mere novice when it came to trading on websites like eBay. Even though he had confidently purchased items over the internet, he had never before offered anything for sale. Now was his big chance to learn.

The sun did not make an appearance that following Monday. A low-pressure trough arcing from the tropical Gulf of Carpentaria down through Central Queensland and Northern New South Wales brought heavy rains into the parched interior. While the farmers were mostly overjoyed at receiving these drought-easing rains, those who rode motorcycles were less than pleased. So, if you cannot ride, you may as well have your pride and joy in for a service, maintenance or repair. Accordingly, a larger than usual number of classic bike enthusiasts had trailered their machines to the workshop that morning.

Even though most of their customers were reluctant to ride in wet weather, Kieran made it into work that morning on his Yamaha SR500. He sloshed his way safely down the laneway and into the workshop. He dismounted with water dripping off his bike and his gear, making puddles on the floor. Michael drove in with Katie, although he had his wet-weather gear with him in case he needed to take any of the motorcycles out for a test ride later in the day. While both men preferred to ride in the dry, neither was deterred by a bit of precipitation.

The old mechanic had the jug boiling by the time the two younger men had stowed their gear in the storeroom. Katie joined them after she had turned on her computer.

'Have any of you ever sold stuff on eBay?' asked the old mechanic while he stirred his mug of tea.

'I've bought stuff, but I haven't sold anything,' replied Katie.

'Same here,' responded Michael. Kieran just nodded in accord with the others.

'But it can't be that hard,' continued Katie. 'What do you want to sell?'

'The Comet.'

'Do you have a minimum price you'd accept?'

'No, not really. I know how much it'd cost to buy if I was in the market for one.'

'How much is that?'

'Between 25 and 30 thousand.'

'I'd start with what it owes you,' interrupted Michael, 'and then double it.'

The old mechanic did some quick mental arithmetic. 'That'd be about 22 grand.'

'If you make that your reserve price, the bidding can start from there.'

'But what if it doesn't get any bids?'

'Then it won't sell,' stated Michael. 'But I'd advertise it on a number of other websites at the same time, rather than having all your eggs in the one basket.'

'Ya need ta take some photos firs',' informed Kieran.

'My phone can do that,' volunteered Katie, 'but you should probably wait for better weather. In the mean-time, I'll do some research for you.'

'And we need to start fixing these motorbikes,' advised Michael, 'or we'll have to sell more than just the Comet.'

In the workshop, amongst the usual assortment of BSAs, Nortons and Triumphs was a pair of Velocettes: a 1953 MAC 350cc and a 1963 Venom 500cc. The 1953 version of the Velocette MAC could trace its history back 20 years. This latest version sported a tube frame, and a swinging arm with fully adjustable rear suspension, as well as having significant improvements made to the clutch and gearbox. Introduced in 1955, the Venom boasted a bi-metal cylinder with a cast-iron liner, high compression piston and a light alloy cylinder head in its 499cc engine. To justify the Venom's higher price when new, it had high quality chrome plating and was finished in black paintwork with gold pin-striping. If the Brough Superior was the Rolls Royce of motorcycles, the Velocette Venom was the E-type Jaguar.

'Who owns the two Velos?' asked the old mechanic after Michael had given him carriage of their work.

'The MAC belongs to a guy by the name of Wayne Hampshire,' replied Michael. 'The Venom's owned by one of his mates in the Velocette Owners' Club.'

'I know Wayne, but I didn't know he had a Velo. I wouldn't mind finding a Venom to restore, but they're pretty rare.'

'As rare as a Comet?' enquired Kieran.

'Not quite, but the Thruxton version's about on par.'

'I thought Thruxton was a Triumph,' suggested Michael.

'They are now,' conceded the old mechanic, 'but back in the day, the original Thruxton was a go-fast version of the Velocette Venom. It earned the name after a modified Venom won its class in the 1964 Thruxton 500-mile endurance race.'

'How do you know everything about these old bikes?'

'I read Mike. And since I discovered the internet, everything's now at my fingertips.'

The two Velocettes were in excellent condition, but both had been tastefully modified, in keeping with their high value, to make ownership easier. They had each been converted to 12 volts and their points' ignition had been swapped for electronic sparks. The Venom also had discreet LED indicators fitted. The two machines were in for an oil change and the MAC needed attention to a noisy tappet.

By mid-morning, Katie had researched how to sell vehicles on eBay and even what the costs would be. Armed with this information, she emerged from her office in time for smoko. The old mechanic looked up from working on the Venom to view his daughter in profile with her now prominent belly.

'Time for smoko, boys,' she called.

The three mechanics gathered around the jug. The old mechanic spoke first. 'I didn't realise your "baby-bump" had grown so much. How many months are you now?'

Katie ran her hands over her slightly protruding stomach. 'Sixteen weeks, give or take. The doctor thinks I'm probably due late August or early September.'

'I reckon he's going to be a football player,' added Michael excitedly, 'he's got a good kick.'

'He? You didn't tell me you were havin' a boy,' exclaimed the old mechanic.

'Actually, we don't know,' corrected Katie. 'Mikey only *thinks* it's a boy because it's been kicking. Girls can kick too, you know.'

'Don' tcha wanna know whacha havin'?' enquired Kieran.

'No! I want it to be a surprise.'

'Do you still get morning sickness?' asked the old mechanic.

'Not much; only when I eat certain foods.'

As the three men began enjoying their morning smoko, Katie continued, 'I found out all you need to know about selling on eBay.'

'All *I* need to know is how much it's going to cost,' professed Michael.

'For vehicles, the listing costs $8.00, plus $14.95 to have a Reserve Price.'

'That's alright,' enthused the old mechanic. 'How much do we pay when it sells?'

'If you sell it, there's a flat fee of $60.00, but you then have the $14.95 recredited to your account.'

The old mechanic thought about it. 'I suppose that's not too bad. But what if you don't sell it?'

'Then you only pay the $22.95.'

'What if we don't set a Reserve?'

'Then it only costs eight bucks, but if it sells, you still pay $60, so it costs the same in the end.'

'If we set a Reserve, it'll weed out the tyre kickers and the gawkers,' suggested Michael.

'When I've searched bikes fer sale on eBay,' affirmed Kieran, 'some set the Reserve too low, and they get stupid bids, and others set it too high, and get none.'

'Do you think 22 grand is too low?' enquired the old mechanic.

'No, but I think 25's too high.'

'That doesn't give us much room to move.'

Kieran did not reply, but merely shrugged his shoulders and smiled, as he stood up to wash his coffee mug. 'I better get back ta work.'

By lunch-time, the rain had stopped and patches of blue could be seen in the north-western sky. Katie was able to walk to the sandwich shop to fetch the lunches without the need to take an umbrella. Her return signalled time for the three mechanics to lay up their tools for lunch.

When everyone had settled down and began eating, the old mechanic suggested, 'If the sun comes out you might be able to take the photos of the Comet this arvo.'

'What do you want to use as a backdrop?' asked Katie.

'You're takin' the photos, what do you suggest?'

'Well, seeing the bike is black, the background should be a lighter colour, so the bike stands out.'

'I think you should use a plain background,' informed Michael, 'so it doesn't detract from the bike. I've seen too many photos where objects in the background are more interesting than the main subject.'

By mid-afternoon, the clouds had cleared revealing a clear blue sky, perfect for taking photographs. The warm autumn sunshine quickly evaporated the standing water. The old mechanic wheeled the Vincent Comet outside into the laneway; the corrugated galvanised steel walls of the workshop making the perfect backdrop for the photography.

'If you want to, we can make a short film of you starting the bike,' proposed Katie, 'and upload it to YouTube. Then we can put a link in the ad.'

'Do you know how to do that?' queried the old mechanic.

'Yeah, of course.'

'But you don't have a movie camera.'

'Da-ad, my phone can take short movies too, you know.'

'And here I was thinking telephones were simply tools to make phone calls.'

'The new smartphones can do everything for you except make a cup of tea and cook dinner,' suggested Michael from behind a Norton Commando.

Katie took about a dozen photographs of the motorcycle from just about every possible angle. She then directed her father in making the short film. The old mechanic was pleased when the motor started first kick.

By knock-off time, she had everything she needed to create a listing for the Vincent Comet on eBay. But that would have to wait for the following day as her father wanted to be involved in the process of creating the ad so he would know for next time.

By 8:30 am the following morning, Katie and the old mechanic had the new eBay listing for the restored 1948 Vincent Comet 500cc, and by the end of the day, bidding was already up to $24,107. The offers crept inexorably higher until, by week's end, it had reached $28,642. During that time, the old mechanic had to field a number of questions about the bike, including from a couple of "scammers" who tried to buy the motorcycle outside the auction for ridiculously low prices. A new wave of bidding over the weekend raised the offer to $29,261, and there it stayed until a flurry just before the end of the auction. The final bid was $29, 759.

On the morning the bidding war concluded, there was a buzz of excitement in the workshop as the four of them huddled around the computer monitor watching the countdown to the end of the auction. When the winning bid was revealed there was a shout of joy from the old mechanic and Kieran, while Katie and Michael hugged and kissed.

'That auction's just saved our bacon,' declared Michael.

'I just hope the winning bidder doesn't try to get out of it,' remarked Katie.

'Can they do that?' the old mechanic asked, suddenly alarmed.

'They can try,' warned Michael. 'But if they do, we can report them to eBay and they can take action against them so they can't do it again.'

As it turned out, the winning bidder was just as excited about his purchase of the Vincent as those who were selling. He telephoned the workshop just after the action ended to arrange transfer of the money and for the collection of the motorcycle. By week's end, the old mechanic was back on eBay looking for the next classic motorcycle to restore.

# Chapter 16

# BONNIE, SWEET BONNIE

The old mechanic was not the only person in the workshop undertaking the restoration of a classic British motorcycle. Kieran, with the help of his father, had been quietly restoring the "basket-case" 1963 Triumph Bonneville T120R. But where the motorcycles being restored in the workshop by the old mechanic were, as nearly as possible, as they would have been when they first left the factory, Kieran's machine was anything but. And whereas the Vincent Comet had been restored for the sole purpose of raising money to keep the business finances liquid, the Triumph Bonneville was being restored purely for the owner's personal satisfaction and enjoyment.

Not wishing to follow the same route of making another café racer like the Yamaha SR500, the modified Bonnie would be remanufactured to look more or less like a standard machine but with a number of changes to enhance performance, while still being sympathetic to its "classic bike" status. Accordingly, most of the "go-fast" modifications would only be evident if the motor was being stripped down.

The engine underwent a complete rebuild with new 750cc barrels, balanced crankshaft, bearings, bearing shells, bushes, seals, high compression pistons, rings, and a lumpier camshaft. The cylinder head was refurbished with new bigger valves, hardened valve seats, guides, heavy-duty springs, tappets, adjusters and seals. All of the fasteners were of stainless steel.

The gearbox received new bearings, bushes, main-shaft, quadrant return spring, plunger and plunger spring, and kick-start return spring. The Lucas K2F magneto was refurbished with a new rotor, 12-volt stator, and Tri-spark electronic ignition. A new primary chain and heavy-duty clutch were installed. A pair of Mikuni CV Carburettors was fitted, along with a set of reverse-cone stainless steel megaphone exhausts.

The frame was braced around the headstock and powder-coated before being fitted with a pair of Ceriani forks with custom-made triple-clamps, matched to a pair of fully-adjustable Ikon rear shocks. A twin leading-shoe vented front brake from a Triumph Trident, and a Trident cush-drive rear hub, were laced to a pair of Akront alloy rims with stainless steel spokes.

The seat was reshaped to add a degree of comfort for a pillion, before being recovered. New instruments included a speedometer, tachometer, oil pressure gauge and ammeter. Flat bars, a set of LED indicators and the controls from a Honda CB750 K3 including the ignition key completed the project.

The only colour that Kieran had been able to discover for the 1963 model Bonneville was cream for the fuel tank and mudguards with black for the oil tank and sidecover. That suited him just fine as it added to the anonymity of the bike. A casual observer would not easily identify that the Bonnie had been "bombed"; only those with a keen eye would notice the modifications to the front brake, the different carbies and the non-standard suspension components. As soon as the frame, fuel and oil tanks, sidecover and the pair of mudguards had been retrieved from the paintshop (the same one used by the old mechanic), reassembly of the motorcycle could begin.

With Easter arriving early that year, the workshop was busy with a greater than average number of classic motorcycle enthusiasts needing their machines prepared in advance of the holiday weekend. In times past, Easter had been the occasion when many motorcycle enthusiasts would gather at Bathurst's Mount Panorama for the Easter Bike Races. But after several years of bad press, when a rowdy, drunken element clashed violently with the police, the races were cancelled. But as so often happens, as the saying goes, when one door closes, another opens. Many classic motorcycle clubs now take the opportunity to hold their national rallies over the four-day holiday long-weekend.

'I wish people wouldn't leave things to the last minute,' whined Michael over his early morning cuppa. 'I'm not sure we'll be able to get all these bikes out the door by knock-off Thursday.'

'We can only do our best Mike,' suggested the old mechanic. 'Poor planning on their part shouldn't constitute an emergency on ours, as the saying goes. If the owners of these old machines can't plan ahead and get their bikes to us in advance, they shouldn't expect us to bust a boiler to finish when they want it.'

'Yeah, well I can't be working late Thursday. Katie and I are going off to Port Stephens for the weekend. We've already booked and paid for the hotel.'

'Good for you,' the old mechanic enthused, 'they've got some great seafood restaurants there.'

'Yeah, Katie wants to go dolphin watching.'

'I hope she doesn't get seasick. What are you doin' on the weekend Kieran?'

'We've got church Frid'y and Sund'y mornin's, but the rest o' the time, me an' dad are puttin' me Bonnie back t'gether. We 'ope to have it finished Mond'y.'

'Really? That hasn't taken long. Is it gonna be standard?'

'Course not!' replied Kieran with a wicked grin, 'It's as hot as.'

'Well, I hope you make it stop as well as it goes,' counselled the old mechanic with a concerned look.

'Yeah we will; we got a vented twin leading-shoe set-up from a Trident.'

'Good!'

The week went quickly, as it often does when everyone is busy. By lunchtime on the Thursday, there were only four customer bikes remaining to be serviced: a 1955 "Squariel" Mark 2, a 1962 Matchless G12CS, a 1967 BSA A65 Thunderbolt and a 1974 Norton Commando Mark 2A.

'Kieran and I can look after these, if you wanna leave early Mike,' suggested the old mechanic over lunch. 'It's a good four-hour drive, if not more if the traffic's heavy.'

'Are you sure?'

'Of course!'

'I don't like leaving you in the lurch.'

'You're not. Now, you and Katie have a good time, and drive safely. Okay?'

'Thanks George.'

When Michael had left, the old mechanic turned to Kieran, 'What say I toss you for who does what bike?'

'Ac'chu'lly, I 'aven't worked on a Square Four Ariel before, c'n I 'ave a go at that firs'?'

The old mechanic looked over at the Ariel with little fondness. 'Are you sure? They're a bugger to work on, and horrible to ride.'

Kieran smiled. 'All the more reason. It'll make me Bonnie feel that much sweeter.'

Kieran wasted little time changing out of his church clothes and into his overalls on Good Friday. His father had already made a start. A pair of Avon sport tyres had already been fitted to the newly constructed wheels. The newly powder-coated frame was sitting on the bikestand waiting for the motor to be installed and bolted in place.

'I've been wonderin' when you'd get 'ere,' intoned John Traeghier.

'It's Good Frid'y – the service was longer 'an usual.'

'Ya gettin' a bit serious about this church thing, arn'cha?'

Kieran did not reply. The two men had already spoken about church and how important it had become in the younger man's life. While his initial motivation for attending had been Lilly, now that he was a Christian, he believed he would continue going, even if he and Lilly broke up, although he was pretty sure that that would never happen. From past experience, the best thing for him to do was to change the subject.

'You've already put the tyres on the rims,' declared Kieran. ''Ave ya balanced 'em yet?'

'Yep, all balanced. They're ready ta be bolted on.'

'Now all we need is somethin' ta bolt 'em on to.'

The father and son duo were used to working together as a team. When John raced and Kieran acted as his mechanic, they had often stripped down and rebuilt the "Black Bomber" after a crash and between races. The only difference here was that there was no strip down necessary or damage to repair.

Where the motor of the Vincent Black Shadow had been painted black, the Bonneville, in common with the Comet, had an unpainted engine. The consequence being that, unless the owner was prepared to keep polishing the crankcases, a coat of clear lacquer was necessary to keep the polished cases from oxidising. Moreover, additional care was required when installing the motor and gearbox into the frame so that the clear coat was not scratched.

By dinnertime, the pair had installed the engine into the frame, and the front forks, triple-clamps, flat-bars, swingarm and rear shock absorbers, both mudguards, and both front and rear wheels, had been attached.

'For the first time, the Bonnie's startin' to look like a real motorbike,' asserted John.

'Yeah, I can't wait to give it a blast,' declared Kieran eagerly.

'I'll toss ya for who goes first.'

'Alright, heads I win, tails you lose.'

'Sounds a plan, man.'

John Traeghier consumed a couple of bottles of beer over dinner, as was his habit, and so he was not in a fit state to resume the rebuild of the Triumph Bonneville after his evening meal. Kieran was happy to spend the evening talking on the phone to Lilly.

For the most part, Saturday mornings were spent asleep in bed, but with a bike to finish, both men were up early and into the garage straight after breakfast. After threading the new wiring loom through the frame, bolting on the twin Mikuni carburettors, and adding all the cables, controls instruments and lights, the morning passed quickly. With just the fuel and oil tanks, sidecover and seat to go, it was time to break for lunch.

'I reckon we're gonna have trouble startin' ya bike,' announced John between mouthfuls of his sandwich.

'Why do ya say that?' asked Kieran.

'Cos we don't 'ave any baseline settin's for the carbies.'

'We c'n set the ignition timin' as per the instructions in the box, and then search the web to get a rough idea of the right jetting.'

'Okay, I'll let you do that.'

While John returned to the garage, Kieran fired up his tablet – a Christmas gift – and quickly searched the internet for the information they needed. Armed with the jettings and needle sizes, he joined his father. John had already bolted on the fuel tank, oil tank, sidecover and seat. Before setting to work on the carburettors and ignition timing, Kieran stood back to admire their work.

'I don't care what anyone says, I reckon it's worth a motza,' he declared.

'Who says it wouldn't be?' replied John, a look of outrage on his face.

'Oh, no-one,' Kieran lied.

The time taken to change the carburettors' needles and jetting and make fine adjustments to the carburation and ignition timing to have the bike running smoothly, took most of the afternoon. But even then, the bike still needed to be ridden out on the open road to test the settings at all speeds and under different loads. John was keen to take the bike for the "shake-down" test, but Kieran urged against taking an unregistered and uninsured bike out onto the roads, especially with double demerits in place over the Easter long weekend.

But having the Triumph Bonneville all but finished and ready to be ridden proved too great a temptation for John. So while Kieran was at church on Easter Sunday morning, his father took the newly restored motorcycle out for a quick ride, with "quick" being the operative word. And, as luck would have it, he was nabbed for speeding, as well as riding an unregistered and uninsured motorcycle. But, adding to the pain in his hip-pocket, his licence was suspended on the spot and the motorcycle impounded.

Kieran returned home from church to the news that his father needed a lift home from the police station, and his Triumph Bonneville had been impounded for one calendar month. The pair was silent on the short journey home; no words were necessary.

As Kieran steered his father's truck into the driveway, a sheepish John spoke, 'Sorry son.'

Kieran looked across to his father, 'That's okay dad.'

'But at least I won the bet.'

Both father and son burst into laughter.

Kieran was quiet when he arrived in to work the following Tuesday morning. Katie and Michael chatted excitedly about their weekend away.

At last the old mechanic turned to Kieran and asked, 'So how'd you go putting the Bonnie back together?'

'We finished it Sat'd'y arvo. It looks sweet as.'

'When do you get it on the road?'

'When I geddit back from the cop shop,' replied Kieran, straight faced.

Everyone turned toward Kieran in alarm.

'What happened?' asked Michael.

# Chapter 17

# BEGGARS CAN'T BE CHOOSERS

Finding another classic British motorcycle to restore was proving more difficult second time around. Those that were worth restoring, were either too expensive in the first place, or they were in such poor condition, there was little value in them. As always, there was a surfeit of BSAs and Triumphs but, like Holdens or Fords amongst car enthusiasts, only the rarest models were worth restoring, and even then, you had to choose carefully.

The old mechanic had made over $18,000 from the sale of the Vincent Comet. Even after taxes and expenses had been taken out, he had still made a handsome profit, but he would need to be careful with the next purchase so that the margins were maintained.

A 1966 Velocette Venom Clubman Mark 2 caught his attention. The machine had been crashed by a previous owner. The current owner had made an attempt at repairing the motorcycle, but it had proved too great an undertaking. According to the advert, the tank was dented, the frame near the headstock was cracked, the front wheel was buckled and the front forks bent. No mention was made of engine damage. Nevertheless, a personal inspection of the machine would be necessary before he made a decision to buy.

The old mechanic had grown used to the sounds of the two 500cc single cylinder motorcycles trundling down the lane to the workshop, Michael on his Norton and Kieran on the

Yamaha. But that morning, a different sound accompanied the familiar pulse from the Bracebridge Street machine. It was an off-beat twin with a louder than normal exhaust noise that roared down the laneway.

He poked his head out of the back door of his small cottage to see Michael and Kieran parking their bikes in the laneway. The younger man was standing next to a cream and black painted Triumph T120R chatting animatedly with his older colleague. The old mechanic wasted little time completing his ablutions so that he could join the two younger men inspecting the new Bonneville.

'I thought you said it'd been impounded for a month,' indicated the old mechanic.

'I did,' agreed Kieran.

'But it's only been just over two weeks.'

'Yeah, well dad's lawyer plays golf with the police inspector. Dad paid a fine and they released me bike. It didn't even hafta go ta court.'

'Did your dad get his licence back?'

'Of course.'

'That's not fair,' moaned Michael. 'If it'd been any one of us who got busted, we would've lost our licence for six months, *and* paid a hefty fine.'

'Yes, well Mike, it's not what you know, but who you know,' proposed the old mechanic.

'Well, it's still not fair.'

'Yeah, well I didn't think it was fair that I lost me bike when it wasn't my fault,' argued Kieran.

A change of subject was in order, so the old mechanic turned to the Triumph.

'You've certainly done a terrific job restoring this Bonnie – it's sweet as can be – I'm really impressed. Where'd you get it painted?'

'Same place you got the Vincent done. Dad knows the bloke pretty good, and 'e was 'appy to give 'im some business.'

The old mechanic's eyes wandered over the machine, noting the Ceriani forks and custom-made triple-clamps, the twin leading-shoe vented front brake and alloy rims with stainless spokes.

'They're top shelf forks, where'd you get 'em?'

'Dad's 'ad 'em in his garage for ages; 'e got 'em when 'e started racin'. 'E was gonna put 'em on the "Black Bomber" but they weren't suitable.'

'Well they certainly don't look out of place on your Trumpy.'

'Now I'm *really* gonna have to sell the Norton and get another bike,' lamented Michael. 'I'll never be able to keep up with Kieran now.'

'Yeah, well, as Kieran's dad's shown, you can only go as fast as the speed limits allow, and that's less than what your Norton can do Mike.'

Michael thought about arguing further, especially with the news that the law did not always apply equally to everyone, but decided against it. He would leave that argument for another day. Several customers had arrived with their bikes and they needed his immediate attention.

So, while Michael dealt with the customers, the old mechanic opened the workshop and Kieran stored both lots of riding gear. The week had been relatively quiet, and so the need to acquire another machine to restore became more of an imperative. But the resurfacing of Michael's dissatisfaction with the performance of his Norton ES2 gave him more food for thought.

With the jug on the boil, Kieran joined the old mechanic to make their early morning cuppa.

'Did you have any difficulty getting the Bonnie registered?'

'A bit,' mused Kieran, 'but once we showed 'em the receipt and a coupla old rego papers, they were 'appy.'

'Yeah, it's always a bit of a trick getting the right papers, especially when machines are so often passed on without any documentation.'

Michael joined the other two mechanics at the tail end of the conversation. 'Have you found another bike to restore yet?'

'There's a wrecked Velo Venom in Sydney, but I'd wanna have a look at it first before I'd commit to it.'

'How much do they want for it?'

'Four and a half.'

'Is it worth it?'

'Yeah, it'd probably be worth that much just in spares.'

'Then what are you waiting for?'

'It's a long way there and back if you only have to get one thing.'

'Then get a load of spares at the same time. Katie was gonna put in an order next week anyway. If you pick them up, it'll save on freight charges.'

The trip to Sydney takes around five hours each way, depending on traffic. As one who is used to the wide-open spaces of the country, and relatively light traffic, the old mechanic had a strong aversion to the congested roads of the "big smoke". Tamworth was like a small country town when compared to Sydney, where even four lane highways were brought to a crawl during peak hour. He could only imagine what it would be like to drive in London, Los Angeles or Tokyo.

Rather than having to cope with peak hour traffic, the old mechanic drove down on the Sunday afternoon, taking advantage of a standing invitation from a widowed cousin of his late wife who lived in the Hills District, to the northwest of the city. She was several years older and quite deaf, but loved having company. She did not have any children of her own, so loved receiving news of her extended family. The old mechanic had not seen her since the wedding, so he was happy to renew the acquaintance and update her with the news that Katie was expecting.

The Velocette Venom Clubman was located in Karuah Street, Strathfield, a short distance from the Rookwood Cemetery in the inner western suburbs of Sydney. The old mechanic arrived at the house a little before 10:00 am. The area was fairly well-to-do, with tree-lined avenues and mostly well-maintained brick and tile houses.

After parking his truck in the street opposite the house, he approached the front door and knocked. After a brief pause when he could hear footsteps and doors being closed, a well-dressed woman in her mid to late fifties opened the glass panelled door.

'Can I help you?' she asked from behind the security screen, an air of disdain in her voice.

'Oh, hello, is Kelvin at home? I rang him about the motorbike he …'

Before the old mechanic could finish, the lady called at the top of her voice, 'Kelvin! There's a man here to see you.' She then slammed the front door, leaving him alone on the front step.

The old mechanic was beginning to feel uncomfortable waiting in front of the closed door. He was contemplating leaving when a short, grey haired man poked his head around the corner of the house. He was dressed in old paint-stained white overalls, and seemed to be the same age as the old mechanic, although he appeared to have had a much harder life.

'Hello there, are you George?'

'Yes, and you must be Kelvin.'

'That's right.'

The two men shook hands. Wordlessly, Kelvin motioned the old mechanic to follow him, back through the side gate and down a paved pathway to a large brick shed at the rear of the property. They passed through a yard meticulously maintained, with billiard-table-smooth lawns, manicured hedges and weedless flower beds. The shed itself was what every red-blooded Aussie bloke could ever dream of having. It was carefully laid out with labelled cardboard boxes arranged on shelves along two walls and, at the back wall, above the workbench, were impeccably cared for tools arrayed neatly on a shadow tool board.

Kelvin approached the rack of shelves on the left side of the shed and pulled out a box with a label describing the contents simple as "Velocette". He then pulled out three other boxes above and beside which were similarly labelled. Finally, from under the workbench, concealed behind a canvass curtain, he retrieved the cracked frame. Once he had everything on the floor, he stood back.

'There you have it: a 1966 Velocette Venom Clubman Mark 2,' he announced.

The old mechanic examined the contents of the boxes and the frame. Everything seemed to be there, including the damaged tank and buckled front wheel. The motor looked as if it was complete and undamaged except for scrape marks on one side. Indeed, it appeared that the Velocette had been in otherwise pristine condition when it had been involved in the accident.

'Did you know the previous owner?' enquired the old mechanic.

'Oh yes, I know him well.' Kelvin looked down at the floor, before mumbling, 'He's my son.'

'What happened?'

Kelvin looked toward the door before lowering his voice. 'My son was riding to work. We'd just restored the Velo, and he was going to show it to all his mates at his office. He was proud as punch. A taxi did a U-turn right in front of him. He clipped the back of it and ended up in the gutter.'

He paused before going on. His voice was now but a whisper. 'He suffered a brain injury. He'll probably never walk or talk again.' A tear began to course down his cheek. 'His mother said to get rid of it. That's why it's for sale.'

'So, the story about it being beyond your ability isn't true.'

Kelvin looked down at the floor. 'No; sorry.'

'You don't need to apologise Kelvin. Why don't you get it repaired first, and then sell it? You'd get a much better price.'

'She who must be obeyed, said to get rid of it *now*.'

'I hate taking advantage of you.'

'You're not. You're the only one to come and see it. Are you still interested?'

'Of course I am. I didn't come all the way from Tamworth for just a look-see.'

'Are you after anything else, beside the Velo?'

'What've you got?' asked the old mechanic, suddenly intrigued.

Kelvin went to another shelf and pulled down a box labelled Ariel, another AJS/Matchless, and two marked Norton. In the various boxes were engine parts, gearboxes, assorted forks, brake drums and fuel tanks. All appeared to be in good condition. Of special interest to the old mechanic were a crankshaft, crankcases, conrod, barrel, piston and head in one of the Norton boxes.

'What're these off?' he asked.

Kelvin examined the parts before announcing, 'Norton Model 19.'

The old mechanic hid his excitement. "Why are you selling all these?'

'She wants me to get rid of everything.'

'How much do you want for them?'

'Make me an offer.'

The old mechanic was in two minds. Without examining everything carefully, he would be unable to determine whether the parts were fully serviceable and how much wear they had been subjected to. Second hand parts, like anything used, are only valuable if they are in good condition, *and* they are needed. At this stage, the only items the old mechanic saw an immediate use for were the Norton parts. But he also did not wish to take advantage of Kelvin.

'I was going to try to knock you down from 45 hundred dollars for the Velo. But would you be interested in five grand for the lot?'

'Five grand? Hmm, okay, after all beggars can't be choosers.'

# Chapter 18

## TESTING TIMES

Katie was beginning to feel increasing levels of discomfort as her bulging tummy continued to grow. She had already met her midwife and her obstetrician, and she had made a tentative booking at the maternity clinic at Tamworth Base Hospital. According to all the tests, the baby was healthy and growing. She still did not know whether she was having a boy or a girl, preferring to keep it a surprise.

She was doing everything right to ensure nothing unforeseen would happen to her unborn child. She was eating a healthy diet devoid of alcohol and junk foods, and had put on little more weight than the weight of the baby. She and Michael went for walks around the neighbourhood each evening after dinner, as time and weather permitted.

From Michael's viewpoint, he thought Katie was the most beautiful creature on the planet. He believed, and told her often, that pregnancy suited her. In his mind, she radiated vitality and delightfulness. But to Katie, she felt in herself that she was fat and ugly. She hated her bulging belly and heavy breasts, and she hated the pimples on her forehead, the first she had had since puberty. No matter what Michael said, she could not feel happy with the way she looked. Halfway there, she said to herself, twenty weeks down and twenty to go.

Ever since her mother was diagnosed with breast cancer, Katie had started examining her own breasts. Even though she was still in her twenties, she was ever conscious that women, younger than she was, could still succumb to the disease, especially if there was a family history.

After showering, she would raise one arm behind her head and, with the fingers of the other arm, examine her opposite breast feeling for a lump. Once completed, she would do the other breast. Sometimes, Michael would catch her in the middle of the examination and want to join in, having become aroused watching her in the mirror from the bedroom. More than once, they ended up in bed making passionate love. Recently, she had begun to produce milk when her nipples were squeezed. Even this was a turn-on for Michael.

Katie was showering while Michael was having breakfast. She did not need to leave early that morning as she would be taking the car to her office job, while Michael rode his bike to the workshop. As she always did, she examined her breasts, although this time, while she was in the shower. But on this occasion, she found a small lump in her left breast. She dried herself and felt for it again. It was still there.

Katie knew the statistics: less than 1 in 10 breast lumps were cancerous, most lumps were nothing but benign cysts, and breast cancer in young, otherwise healthy women was rare. But there was still a chance, especially when there was a family history of the disease. She already had her regular appointment with Dr Bailey the following Monday afternoon, so she decided that she would speak to her about it then. She did not tell Michael.

The time passed slowly, as it always does when you are waiting for something to occur. It seems to pass even more slowly when you cannot, or will not, tell those whom you love what is troubling you. Eventually, the time came. She had already seen the nurse and the sonographer, so she knew that the baby was growing as it should. She even had a sonagraph of the baby to show Michael and her father. Katie sat nervously in the surgery sitting area, waiting for her name to be called.

'Katie Edwards!'

Katie leapt up from her chair and almost ran to the doctor's surgery.

Even before she sat down, she blurted out, 'I think I have cancer,' and, 'I don't want to lose my baby.' The pent up emotions of the past few days suddenly came flooding to the surface and she burst into tears, and slumped into the chair next to the doctor's desk.

Dr Bailey took some tissues from the box on the shelf above her desk and handed them to her sobbing patient. When she had calmed down enough to be questioned, she asked, 'What makes you think you have cancer?'

'I found a lump in my left breast.'

'What makes you think it's cancerous?'

'Because I have a family history of breast cancer.'

'How old are you Katie?'

'Twenty-five.'

'You know the chances that someone as young and as healthy as you are, of having breast cancer are less than half of one percent? And the fact that you're pregnant makes the chances even smaller.'

Katie was unmoved by the statistics. 'Yes, but there's still a chance,' she retorted.

'Okay, let me have a look.'

Katie disrobed and lay on the examination bed. The doctor felt for the lump in Katie's breast, before checking under her arm for her lymph nodes. She then undertook a complete examination, including the positioning of the baby.

'You can get dressed now.'

While the doctor washed her hands, Katie climbed down off the bed and got dressed.

When they were both seated Doctor Bailey asked, 'How many months are you now?'

'I'm twenty weeks.'

'Your baby seems fine. But, you're right, there is a lump, and your lymph nodes under your left arm are slightly inflamed. But that still doesn't necessarily mean you have cancer.'

'What else could it mean then?'

'It could be just a cyst. The hormones coursing through your body, the ones that caused your morning sickness, can also cause a cyst to form. But to be sure, I want you to see a surgeon who'll take a biopsy of the lump and then we can decide if we need to do anything.'

'Nothing'll happen to my baby, will it?'

'No, of course not, your baby should be just fine.'

'If it's cancer, will I have to have a mastectomy?'

'Katie, let's cross that bridge when we come to it. Okay?'

'Should I tell Mikey?'

'Is he the father?'

'Yes, of course.'

'That's up to you. But if I was in your shoes, I'd want the father of my baby to know about anything that could possibly affect its health.'

Katie did not go back to her office job after the doctor's appointment. She instead returned home via the butcher's and the green grocer's. If she had unpleasant news to tell Michael, it would be better received, she surmised, received on a full stomach. While Michael knew that his wife had an appointment with her GP, he was blissfully unaware that anything could be wrong, so well did she hide the truth about her breast lump from him.

The smell of the roasting leg of lamb assaulted his olfactory senses as soon as Michael entered the unit, a little before 5:00 pm. Of all the red meats, lamb was his favourite, and of all the ways to cook lamb, roasting reigned supreme. Katie had learned very early that the way to her man's heart was through his stomach. Before he had removed his riding gear, she met him at the front door with a long kiss and an even longer hug.

When they drew apart, she asked, 'How was your day, my darling?'

'Like every other day when you're not around. Gee I miss you when you're not at the workshop.'

'Well, we have just one more day, and then we can spend the weekend together.'

'In bed?' Michael enquired hopefully.

'Anywhere you like.'

'What's that I can smell cooking?'

'Roast leg of lamb.'

'Who's coming to dinner? Are we having guests?'

'No, just you and me, and our baby,' she replied, patting her bulging belly.

'Oh, and speaking of babies, how did your doctor's appointment go?'

'Yeah, good, I'll tell you all about it after dinner.'

Michael could tell that everything was not as it seemed. He knew that she was hiding something, but decided to wait. He also knew from past experiences that, if there was anything he *needed* to know, Katie would tell him at the appropriate time; forcing the issue would not bring a good outcome.

Even though she was not allowed to drink alcohol, Katie had learned from her mother how to make a delicious red wine sauce to smother the meat when it was served. Michael carved the leg while she made the sauce in the pan juices. Normally she would use a bottle of "rough red", but on this occasion, she opened a bottle of 2012 Tulloch Shiraz from the Hunter Valley. What she did not use for the sauce, she would serve to Michael with the lamb.

The dinner went down a treat. The meat and vegetables were cooked to perfection, and the wine was the ideal complement. For dessert they had compote of peaches with fresh cream. The meal was absolutely delicious, just as Katie had planned.

As Katie stood to clear the table and Michael was finishing his peaches, he asked, 'So, you gonna tell me *now* what the doctor said?'

'After we clean up and stack the dishwasher.'

'Katie, what did the doctor say?'

Katie continued to clear the table, not wanting to make eye contact with Michael. He stood and grasped hold of his wife's wrists, 'Katie!'

Katie turned toward her husband before busting into tears. She fell into his arms, her body wracked with sobs, the pent-up emotions overflowing. He led her over to the sofa where she sat down. He grabbed a box of tissues and joined her. It would be several minutes before she regained her composure enough to speak.

'I've got a lump … in my breast … I hafta have a biopsy next week to see if it's cancer.'

'Damn it to hell Katie, why didn't you tell me? When did you find the lump?'

'Last Thursday.'

'Why didn't you tell me then?'

''Cause I didn't want you to worry.'

'Damn! Does the doctor think it's cancer?'

'She wouldn't say. She said she'd prefer to wait for the biopsy results.'

'What about the baby?'

'She said it should be all right. But if it *is* cancer, I don't want to do anything that'll harm it.'

'What do you mean?'

'Well, if it's cancer, I don't want any treatments like radiation or chemo therapy if it could harm the baby.'

'But if it *is* cancer, don't you think your health is more important than the baby's?'

'Mikey, I've already lost one baby; I'm not gonna lose another one.'

'Isn't that a decision we should be making together? The baby is ours and we belong to each other. Any decisions we make, should be made together.'

Michael could sense that his wife was only half listening, so he added, 'Why don't we wait until you get the results of the biopsy; then we can decide what to do. With any luck it'll be nothing, and we'll have worried ourselves sick for no reason.'

Michael rose early the following morning to get ready for work. He had not slept very well; thoughts of Katie and the baby kept his mind working throughout the night. At least his wife slept fitfully. Keeping the secret for so long had left her drained.

They had agreed to keep the news from anyone else until they knew for certain. They felt that telling others, and especially Katie's father and Michael's mother, would cause them both a level of anxiety that was not necessary until they knew for sure whether the lump was cancerous.

The weekend dragged past, even though they both tried to keep occupied. Michael had told the old mechanic that he would not be coming into the workshop the following Monday as Katie needed to have a "minor procedure" in the Outpatient's Clinic at the Tamworth Base Hospital. He assured him that everything was fine and that there was no need to be concerned. If only he felt the same way.

Katie lay nervously on the examination table in the Clinic surgery. The biopsy would be done under local anaesthetic with the aid of ultrasound to exactly locate the lump. She felt particularly vulnerable with her left breast exposed. A Nursing Sister prepared for the procedure by swabbing the site with a sterile solution. The fluid was cold adding to Katie's discomfort. She closed her eyes.

The surgeon came and stood over Katie. 'Good morning Katie. There's going to be a slight sting when I insert the needle with the anaesthetic, but you shouldn't feel too much discomfort after that; if you do, please tell me.'

The "slight sting" felt like a white-hot needle searing her flesh. She winced at the pain.

'Are you okay?' asked the surgeon.

'Yeah, I think so,' she lied.

Katie did not feel the biopsy needle going in, and before she knew it, the operation was over.

'When will I know if the lump is cancer?' she asked the surgeon before he left the room.

'Two or three days; I'll send a report to Dr Bailey.'

Katie left the hospital with Michael late that morning. After dropping her off at their unit in Banjo Creek and collecting his riding gear, he continued on to the workshop.

# Chapter 19

# NO SUBSTITUTE FOR CUBES

The old mechanic had already made a start restoring the Velocette Venom Clubman. As far as the models were concerned, the Clubman stood midway between the Standard Venom and the racing version, the Venom Thruxton. It was designed specifically for the average "club man" to be able to compete in their local motorcycle club events, while still being available to commute to work during the week.

Over the standard model, the Clubman was fitted with a GP2 Amal carburettor, a manually controlled BTH racing magneto (in place of the Lucas unit) and a close-ratio gearbox, with the compression ratio raised to 9.3 to 1. The Venom Clubman dispensed with the glass fibre engine enclosure and instead made a feature of highly polished crankcase and gearbox castings. Supplied with rear-set controls, lowered handlebars and a steering damper, the Clubman also had a range of optional accessories including a megaphone exhaust silencer, rev counter and light alloy wheel rims.

For the 1966 model year, the Venom was upgraded to the Mark 2 specifications, which had the Thruxton front forks fitted with rubber gaiters, a twin leading shoe front brake and narrowed mudguards, combined with a new exhaust design giving it a more modern sports motorcycle look. It was this model that the old mechanic had acquired.

When restoring a classic motorcycle for profit, rather than for personal use, it is imperative to keep the machine as close as possible to the original specification. Many classic motorcycle aficionados prefer originality over restoration, indeed, original patina of painted surfaces, including fuel tanks is nearly always preferred over an item that has been freshly painted.

The old mechanic had already identified a number of changes previous owners had made to this Venom Clubman. For a start, it had been converted to 12 volts and the spark was now produced electronically rather than by contact breaker points. It also had a Mark 2 Amal Concentric carburettor fitted in place of the GP2. He guessed these changes had been made to make the bike more "civilised" when riding in the confines of the Sydney metropolitan area. Normally, he would simply order a replacement GP2 carbie to fit to the Velo, but with the slide of the Aussie dollar over the last year or more, a new item would cost in the vicinity of $900.00, which was a good chunk of the profit he hoped to make. He also considered that going back to 6 volts and points ignition a retrograde step.

As he always did, he stripped the motor down to see what, if any, damage had been incurred in the accident or if there had been any abnormal wear to the various mechanical components. Other than the aforementioned scrapes on the chain-case, the inner workings of the Velocette 499cc motor appeared to be all new. The pistons, rings, valves, valve springs, tappets, pushrods, bearings, in fact everywhere he looked everything was brand spanking new.

He suddenly felt very sad for Kelvin. In one moment of poor judgement by the driver of the taxi and the possible inattention by the rider, he had lost his son, as well as the very thing they had both worked so hard together to put back on the road; a very much loved Velocette Venom Clubman. But where machines are easily repaired or replaced, people are not.

Michael had been absent during the Monday morning. He had taken Katie to the Outpatients' Clinic at Tamworth Base Hospital for a "minor procedure" that had apparently nothing to do with her pregnancy. The old mechanic could only imagine what that could be. Michael had appeared distracted on the previous Friday, and things seemed little better when he arrived for work just before lunch on the Monday.

When he emerged from the storeroom where he had deposited his riding gear, the old mechanic collared him, 'Is Katie alright?'

'Yeah, she's fine; a little bit sore, but she's okay.'

'What'd she have done?'

'It was just a minor procedure. She should be alright to come in to work tomorrow.'

The old mechanic was not entirely happy with the answer, but he did not want to push the issue. While Katie was still his daughter, she was now also Michael's wife and so, technically, no longer his responsibility. So, he let it rest, for now.

The old mechanic had sent the Velocette's damaged forks to Pro-tech Suspension Specialists in Sydney to have them straightened and replated, while the tank had been sent to his painter in South Tamworth to be repaired and repainted. The front wheel rim was damaged beyond economical repair, so he salvaged what he could and ordered a new alloy rim. The tyre itself was still almost new. The front mudguard was bent, but repairable.

With Kieran's help welding, they fixed the crack in the frame. After measuring the frame to ensure it was straight, he spray painted the welded section to conceal the repair. With new headstock bearings, it was ready to go.

The various minor controls that had been damaged in the collision – the left side foot-peg, foot-brake, handgrip, bar-end mirror and clutch lever – were either replaced with generic items held or ordered from their classic bike parts supplier. The scrapes on the chain-case were polished out.

With the Velocette restoration now stalled, awaiting new or repaired parts, the old mechanic turned his attention to the contents of the various boxes of parts he had brought back from his trip to Sydney. His immediate priority was the box marked "Norton Parts". According to Kelvin, the parts belonged to a Norton Model 19, but he had not specified whether they belonged to a motor pre- or post-war. The difference was important because the bore and stroke of the pre-war Model 19 was 79mm x 120mm, making a capacity of 588cc. The post-war Model 19, on the other hand, had a bore and stroke of 92mm x 113mm, making a capacity of 596cc. The difference on the road was that the post-war motor was more flexible having more useable power.

The old mechanic grabbed his vernier callipers and measured the bore of the barrel. He grunted with satisfaction when he found that the parts he had purchased were from a post-war Model 19. While the bore and stroke of Michael's ES2 was 79mm x 100mm, it would not be a simple matter of bolting on the larger components to increase the capacity from 490cc to 596cc, but the resulting machine, with appropriate modifications, would make a better road-bike. By mid-afternoon, he had thought out a plan of attack; all he needed was Michael's agreement, and his motorbike.

The old mechanic filled up the electric jug, calling to his two co-workers, 'You two stoppin' for smoko?'

Kieran did not need a hurry-up, having just completed servicing an early model Triumph T100. Michael was up to his elbows in grease and oil servicing a BSA A7.

'Come on Mike, the jug's boiled.'

'Hang on; I need to wash my hands first.'

When Michael eventually joined the others, he needed to boil the jug again. When he had made his tea and sat down, the old mechanic turned to him.

'How'd ya like a bigger bike?'

'It'd be nice, but we can't afford it now. And besides, Katie doesn't want me to get rid of the old Norton.'

'What if we could have two for the price of one?'

'I don't get you.'

'Well, when I went down to Sydney to collect the Velocette Venom Clubman, the vendor had some boxes of spare parts he had to get rid of. The boxes contained spares for various Ariel, AJS and Matchless motorcycles, and there were two boxes of Norton parts. Have you heard of a Norton Model 19?'

'Yeah, it's a 600 single.' Michael was beginning to understand what the old mechanic was getting at.

'With a bit of work, the Model 19 parts can be made to fit the crankcases of your "Easy 2".'

'How much work's required?'

'I reckon we could have it done in a few days, in between everything else. What do you think?'

'How much is it gonna cost?'

'I haven't worked that out yet, but I reckon it wouldn't be much more than a coupla hundred bucks. And besides, if we sell the rest of the parts on eBay, we could recoup the lot.'

'Could we take it back to standard if it doesn't work out?'

'Believe me Mike, it'll work. You'll have the best ES2 in the country.' Michael remained hesitant, so the old mechanic turned to Kieran. 'What do you reckon, Kieran?'

'As me ol' man says, "There's no substitute for cubes". Your ol' Norton'll still look like a 500, but it'll have heaps more grunt, just like my Bonnie looks like a 650. But when you give 'em a squirt, they'll embarrass almost anythin' else.'

'It could certainly do with some more poke,' agreed Michael.

'And it'll be much better two-up if Katie wants to go for a ride too,' enthused the old mechanic.

Michael smiled. 'We'll probably need to attach a sidecar when the baby arrives.'

'A sidecar won't be a problem with a 600 single. So, is it a goer?'

'Sure, why not. But I'll need a lift to work when Katie's got the car for her other job.'

The old mechanic and Kieran replied together, 'No problem.'

Katie arrived for work the following morning, just after Michael on his old Norton. Kieran had already parked his Triumph Bonneville and had filled the jug for their first cuppa of the morning, while the old mechanic dealt with some customers.

When the four came together, the old mechanic's first concern was for his daughter. 'How did yesterday go, Sweetheart? Are you feelin' better now?'

'Yeah, and I'll be better still once I get the test results.'

'What results are those?' asked the old mechanic innocently.

'Blood tests,' interjected Michael, 'to see if she's anaemic.'

The old mechanic was still not entirely happy with the answer but, he thought, what more could he do? He hated being kept in the dark about Katie, so he had to trust them that they would inform him if he had a "need to know".

So he turned to Kieran, 'Does your dad's fabrication business have a machine shop?'

'Yeah, of course; whad'ja 'ave in mind?'

'We need to get the spigot on the 19's barrel machined to take the later ES2 head, and we need to machine the head to suit the larger barrel.'

''E did some machinin' on me Bonnie motor, so I'm sure 'e'd be 'appy to 'elp with Mike's ol' Norton.'

'What other work needs to be done to the motor,' asked Michael, his reluctance of the previous afternoon appearing to have vanished.

'When we get your old crankshaft out, we'll need to remove the flywheel and the alternator drive, and get them pressed into the 19's crank in place of the generator drive. Once that's done, we need to balance the crank.'

'Will we need new bearings to fit the different crankshaft?'

'No, the old ones should be fine, unless you've worn them out, of course. But we'll need spacers for the pushrod tubes; after that we'll need to gear it up a bit to take advantage of the larger capacity.'

'What about the clutch?'

'No, we put in some bonded clutch plates when we built it up in the first place, so that should be okay. But we'll probably need to rejet the carbie to take advantage of the stronger bottom end, as well as more top-end power.'

John Traeghier was happy to help with the transformation of the ES2 motor, but when asked to quote on the cost, he merely replied, 'Mate's rates.' Michael never did get a bill for the work he did.

The report from the pathology lab arrived on Dr Bailey's desk late on Wednesday afternoon. Normally a patient would need to make an appointment to receive the results, but on this occasion, the doctor called her patient. Katie took the call just after she arrived home from work.

'Hello.'

'*Hello Katie, it's Dr Sarah Bailey.*'

'Hello Dr Bailey, have you got the report?'

'*Yes Katie, and it's good news, the lump is benign, as we hoped. You can rest easy now.*'

'Thanks Dr Bailey.'

# Chapter 20

# KEEPING UP WITH KIERAN

The old mechanic had not slept well. He knew that Katie's "minor procedure" and "tests" had nothing to do with low iron levels in her bloodstream, even though the possibility during pregnancy was very real. Thoughts kept swirling around in his head about what could be wrong with her. He remembered without any real pleasure his own wife and all the tests she had to endure before she was diagnosed with breast cancer. His heart sank at the thought that Katie might have to go through with the same regimen.

Unable to sleep any longer, he rose early. The sky was still dark outside, even though daylight saving had already finished. He had a mild headache from a lack of sleep and his eyes felt like they were full of grit. After a couple of paracetamol tablets and a splash of cold water on his face, he felt better, but not by much. He switched on the radio to catch the latest news while he made his customary tea and toast for breakfast, but the news headlines made him feel worse.

Being mid-autumn, the weather was perfect for riding motorcycles; Goldilocks weather they call it – not too hot and not too cold. All three mechanics had been busy in the preceding weeks; the two younger ones repairing and servicing a host of classic British motorcycles, while the old mechanic had been busy restoring the Velocette. Life could not get much better, or so it would seem.

The sun had just risen above the horizon when the old mechanic opened the workshop, and he was busy pulling

Michael's Norton ES2 apart when the two younger mechanics rode down the laneway together; Kieran at the controls of his Triumph Bonneville, with Michael riding pillion.

'Gee that thing's got some stick, even two-up,' declared Michael as he jumped off. 'I hope my Norton'll be able to keep up with you when it's finished.'

'My Bonnie'd be even better if it 'ad a five-speed box,' lamented Kieran. 'Right now, that's the only thing 'oldin' 'er back.'

'Well, you have to have *some* kind of handicap.' When Michael realised that the old mechanic had already pulled the motor out of his Norton he asked, 'What time did you get here?'

'A bit after six, why?'

'How come? Couldn't you sleep?'

'As a matter o' fact, no. Come with me, I wanna talk.'

'Hang on a sec; I'll just put me gear in the storeroom.'

The old mechanic waited in Katie's office while Michael deposited his jacket, helmet and gloves in the storeroom. When he joined the old mechanic, the door closed behind him.

'I don't want any crap from you Mike, what's wrong with Katie?'

'There's nothing wrong,' replied Michael, evenly.

'Bulldust! You don't go into hospital for a "medical procedure" just to check if someone's anaemic. What's wrong with her?'

The old mechanic's face was turning red and his raised voice carried through the closed door and out into the workshop, causing one of their regular customers to look up from discussing his Norton Dominator 7 with Kieran. Michael had never seen his father-in-law so angry or upset.

In a lowered voice, he replied, 'Katie found a lump.'

The old mechanic's heart sank again. 'Why didn't you tell me?'

'I didn't tell you, because Katie didn't tell me. I didn't find out 'til after she'd been to see her GP.'

'Has she got the results of the test yet?'

'Yeah, her doctor rang late yesterday; it's a benign cyst.'

'Oh, thank God. Well, I want you to tell me if ever anything like that happens again. Okay?'

'Look George, even if we had told you that she'd found a lump, what would you've done?'

The old mechanic did not reply, so Michael continued. 'You would've worried. And as it turned out, you would've worried for nothing. Katie may be your daughter, but she's *my* wife, and so she's *my* responsibility.'

The old mechanic remained silent for a long moment. A tear began to course down his right cheek. 'I'm sorry Mike,' he mumbled.

'I'm sorry too George.'

'You know, she's all I have left. I don't wanna lose her.'

'You won't lose her George, or me, or the baby.'

'Thanks Mike.'

'Come on, I need a cuppa.'

'Me too.'

When the old mechanic had removed the Norton 500's crankshaft, he packed it and the head with the Model 19's crank and barrel into a box and took them to John Traeghier's metal fabrication premises in South Tamworth. John was tied up in a meeting with his accountant, so he had delegated one of his best tradesmen to help with the machining of the head and the barrel, and making the changes to the two crankshafts.

By Friday afternoon, the work had been completed and the old mechanic returned to pick everything up. John met him as he arrived.

'G'day George.'

'Hello John, thanks for doin' this work for me.'

'It's my pleasure. What are the parts from?'

'The barrel and one of the cranks are from a Norton Model 19, and the head and other crank is from Michael's ES2. I'm gonna make the 500 into a 600 so Mike can keep up with Kieran.'

John laughed. 'I've been tryin' ta keep up with Kieran ever since 'e got 'is bike licence. Hey, d'ya like 'is Triumph Bonneville?'

'Of course, it's a credit to you both. What are you riding now that you've given up racin'?'

'I've got my eye on a Commando 850 Mk3, the one with the electric leg.'

'Well just remember that the electric start is one of the weaknesses of that model.'

'Yeah, that's what Kieran said. "E gave me the full rundown of what to look for.'

'What're you gonna do with your old "black bomber"?'

''I already flogged it on eBay. Some bloke from Brizzie wanted to build one up to race, and saw mine as a way of short-cuttin'.'

'D'ya miss racin'?'

'Nah, been too busy, what with the business and restorin' Kieran's Bonnie; I 'aven't 'ad time ta scratch meself.'

'Well, I better get goin'.'

'Yeah, an' I've got work ta do meself. See ya later.'

'Yeah, thanks John, see ya.'

The old mechanic returned to the workshop just as the other two mechanics were packing up their tools. With no transport for himself, Michael did not wish to keep Kieran waiting, so he was relieved when the old mechanic arrived.

'I've done all the invoices,' advised Michael. 'The owners of the Dommie 7 and the A65 said they'd be here before 4:30, so they should be here soon.'

'Thanks Mike.'

'Are ya 'appy with the machinin' job?' asked Kieran.

'Yeah, so far, but I won't know for sure until I put everything back together. I spoke to your dad; he said he was thinkin' of gettin' a Commando.'

'Yea, I wanted 'im ta get a Bonnie like mine, but 'e said 'e wouldn't be able ta keep up with me.'

'A Commando'll certainly give you a run for your money.'

Kieran gave a mischievous grin. "E won't 'ave a 'ope.'

'Well, we'll see you Monday,' interrupted Michael.

'Yeah, 'avagoodweekend George,' called Kieran.

'Yeah, see youse.'

The old mechanic arrived early for work Monday morning, but not because he could not sleep. Indeed, he had had the most restful weekend he could remember. No, he arrived early to get a start on putting Michael's ES2 back together. He was excited at the prospect of how good the larger capacity motor might be, and how much it would transform the motorcycle.

Even though he could easily have used the original bearings in the new motor, he decided to renew everything while he had it stripped down. The only downside was that Michael would need to bed everything in again as the engine was run-in, but that was a small price to pay for what was essentially, a new motor.

Before he started the rebuild, the old mechanic needed to rebalance the modified crankshaft. This was done using a jig to see where in its rotation the shaft is heaviest; once that was determined, weight was either added to or taken away from the flywheel. Because the new motor was using the crankshaft from the Norton Model 19, it already had the heavier flywheel attached, so very little effort was required to make it balance.

The original head of the ES2 had previously been ported, fitted with larger valves and the head flowed to ensure gases an easy pathway into and out of the combustion chamber. By lunchtime, the old mechanic had the motor back together, ready to be fitted back into the frame. Now the only thing holding up the rebuild was that the larger engine sprocket had not yet arrived. While he could have fitted the larger sprocket after the motor was reinstalled, it was an easier job to do it with the motor on the workbench.

With his two projects now stalled, the old mechanic volunteered to do the lunchtime sandwich run. While Katie was still willing and able to collect the lunches, she happily deferred to her father, on this occasion. His return signalled that it was time for lunch.

While the jug boiled, Michael enquired, 'When do I get my bike back?'

'When the sprocket arrives from the Chain Gang,' advised the old mechanic. 'With any luck, that'll be tomorrow morning.'

'I'm looking forward to taking it for a ride.'

'Well, just remember, it'll need to be run-in again, so no giving it a fist-full.'

'Yeah, I know.' Michael turned to Kieran. 'Our duel will have to wait just that little bit longer.'

Kieran smiled, 'Classic bikes at 50 paces.'

The sprocket arrived with the post the following day. By lunchtime the old mechanic had the bike running, and by mid afternoon, he had rejetted the carburettor so that it was running smoothly across the rev range and under load. He was surprised at how much of a difference the larger capacity made to how the bike accelerated and cruised; where once it was just another 500cc British single, now it was a powerhouse.

Michael met his father-in-law when he arrived back at the workshop after taking the Norton for its final test run. 'How is it?'

'It's fantastic! It's got more grunt than my Dommie and almost as much power. The five-speed box is a terrific addition to it. I'm almost inclined to order one for my bike.'

'But your Dommie wouldn't be standard.'

'So? I bought my bike to ride, not to showcase. And besides, it's not standard now. If I ever planned to sell it, I could still swap it back, although the buyer would probably see the new box as a plus anyhow.'

By this time, Kieran had joined the others, hearing the discussion about the gearbox. 'Do they make five-speed boxes for me Bonnie?'

'The later models have a five-speed standard, but I don't know if they'll retrofit into your gearbox; you can always investigate. I know they make them for Norton Commandos, so your dad will be able to upgrade his if he goes down that track.'

'Don't tell 'im that, I wanna keep me winnin' edge.'

'You know Kieran, it's not the bike that makes the rider, it's the rider that makes the bike. A good rider on a bad bike will always beat a bad rider on a good bike.'

Kieran smiled, 'Yeah, but a good rider on a good bike will beat 'em both.'

# Chapter 21

## I'VE BEEN EVERYWHERE MAN

With Michael's bike back on the road, the old mechanic was beginning to look for things to do, so the straightened front forks off the Velocette Venom arrived just at the right time from Pro-tech Suspension Specialists. The forks were not only straightened, but new seals were fitted after the originals were damaged in the process of straightening. He was very pleased with the quality of the finished items and made a mental note to use them again in the future.

The new alloy rim arrived soon after the forks, so it was now time to rebuild the front wheel. In the storeroom, the old mechanic found the Mercer Gauges that Kieran had returned after building the wheels for his Triumph Bonneville. The jig that he had once constructed when they restored Michael's Norton had long since been cannibalised for some other use, so he had to make another from scraps of timber.

Meanwhile, the two younger mechanics had been busy with their own work: Michael servicing a Matchless G12 twin, and Kieran an Ariel FH Huntmaster. While both machines bore similar specifications – 646cc overhead valve vertical twin engines – the two motorcycles were otherwise very different. The Matchless motor had bore and stroke dimensions of a relatively square 72mm x 79.3mm, where the Ariel (which had a BSA A10 derived motor) had very under square dimensions of 70mm x 84mm. But, where the slow revving BSA compensated by weighing less than the Matchless, the

Ariel weighed significantly more. It was no surprise then that the Ariel was the preferred mount for attaching a sidecar.

The three mechanics had just broken for lunch when the sound of a vertical twin motorcycle made its way down the laneway outside. But rather than being a 650 overhead valve motor propelling it, the machine was of a modern double overhead camshaft design with a capacity of 865cc. The old mechanic met Jim Browning as he alighted from his motorcycle.

'There's no doubt about you, your timing's impeccable.'

'Is it lunchtime already?' asked a smiling Jim as he took off his gloves and helmet.

'Yeah, d'ya wanna cuppa?'

'You know me, never say no.'

Jim helped himself to the milk in the refrigerator while the old mechanic spooned coffee and sugar into the spare mug. When everyone was seated, the old mechanic questioned their visitor.

'So what brings you here? D'ya wanna go for another ride on the weekend?'

'I wanna go for another ride, but not this weekend,' replied Jim.

'I don't wanna make plans too far ahead in case I have to cancel them. What've you got in mind?'

'Have you seen the latest edition of *Cycle Torque*?'

'I've seen it, but I haven't read it yet. Why, does it have a review of the latest and greatest out of Europe or Japan?'

'Actually no, it's got a review of the latest and greatest out of New Zealand.'

'I didn't know New Zealand made motorbikes, well, at least not since John Britten passed away.'

'It's not motorbikes that the Kiwis do well at, it's motorbike holidays.'

Jim opened his copy of *Cycle Torque* to a double page spread near the back of the magazine. The headline read: **CLASSIC FLY-RIDE**. The accompanying article was about an organised touring holiday where riders fly to New Zealand aboard a DC-3 Dakota and then tour both the North and South Islands by Royal Enfield over the next fourteen days. Riders also have the option of taking their own classic motorcycle if they wish.

In the North Island, the riders would be taking in a number of organised ride days at various race tracks including Pukekohe Motor Racing Circuit and Taupo Motorsport Park in Waikato, before heading to the Hampton Downs Motorsport Park to see the Barry Sheene Festival of Speed. Visits to the hot springs at Rotorua and cruising Lake Taupo were also on the itinerary. After being ferried to the South Island, the tour takes in some of the best roads and scenery the country has to offer. The tour ends in Christchurch where the Dakota will be waiting to fly participants back to Australia.

After skimming through the article, the old mechanic asked, 'How much?'

'If you ride their bike, it's five thousand Kiwi dollars, twin share.'

'What if I use my own bike?'

'It's three grand, plus a grand Aust to ship your bike there and back.'

'When is it?'

'The Barry Sheene Festival of Speed is on the last weekend in October, so you've got about five months to save up.'

'Hmm, I've always wanted to tour New Zealand.'

'Me too. So whad'ya reckon?'

'And they say late spring and early autumn's the best time to go.'

'Exactly!' exclaimed Jim enthusiastically.

'But I've always dreamed of riding through Great Britain. There're a lot more circuits to see and museums to visit in the Ol' Dart.'

'But it hasn't got New Zealand's scenery, and it's a whole lot cheaper across "The Ditch", and closer.'

'Yeah, I know. Let me think about it, okay?'

'Okay, but don't think too long. I rang 'em up and they said places are fillin' up fast.'

'Are you goin' anyway?'

'I've already booked.'

'But you don't have a classic bike!'

'My bike's a modern classic,' replied Jim with a mischievous grin. 'Well, I best be on me way.'

'Yeah, and we've got work to do,' declared Michael.

After Jim left, Michael approached the old mechanic, 'Are you really interested in that holiday?'

'Of course I'm interested, why?'

'Oh, just wondering. If I had to pick a "once-in-a-lifetime" holiday and the choice was either New Zealand or Great Britain, I'd go where I'd always dreamed of going.'

'Yeah, and if time and money wasn't an issue, I'd probably choose the same. But unless you want to loan me the cash and give me three months off to spend it, I'm gonna hafta compromise.'

By early afternoon, the old mechanic had finished lacing the spokes and truing the new front wheel of the Velocette. As he had anticipated, the brake linings were almost new, so too the brake cables. The only item requiring his attention now was the bent front mudguard.

Of all the tasks required to undertake in the restoration of a classic British motorcycle, panel beating was the old mechanic's least favourite. But other than buying a reproduced item out of India, or make one from scratch himself, the only way that he would be able to obtain what he needed was to repair the item at hand. The one saving grace was that the mudguard was neither cracked nor creased.

The old mechanic found his panel beating tools – two unusually shaped hammers and a variety of curved solid metal dollies – in the storeroom. He selected the dolly whose shape roughly coincided with the inside curve of the guard and clamped it tightly in the vice attached to the workbench.

Where the mudguards from the Vincent Black Shadow that he restored the previous year were made from aluminium alloy, the guards from the Velocette were made from steel. So, while they were harder to damage, they were also harder to repair. So, in addition to the panel beating tools, he needed heat. A propane gas bottle with a torch attachment would provide the heating necessary, and a leather glove would offer the required protection for his hand.

With his gloved left hand holding the steel guard over the dolly, and the other hand alternately armed with the propane torch or one of the hammers, he heated and tapped away at the mudguard to straighten it and free it of its dents. He laboured thus all afternoon. By the time the others were ready to leave for the day, he had removed the dents and straightened the guard to a satisfactory level. Now all that was required were a couple of coats of paint.

After giving the front mudguard a coat of primer, the old mechanic closed the workshop and strode the 50 or so paces to his empty house. Since Katie had moved out, he had started eating at his local club on a semi-regular basis; the bistro at the South Tamworth Bowling Club had cheap meals for seniors, Monday to Thursday nights. Indeed, it was sometimes cheaper and easier for him to eat out, than it was to buy the necessary ingredients and cook for himself.

After a quick shower and change of clothes, he had about half an hour to kill, so he turned on his laptop computer. Once it had booted up, he searched for the on-line motorcycling magazine: *Cycle Torque*. In the latest edition, he found the article that Jim had shown him at lunchtime. This time he read the article right through. He went to dinner at the Bowling Club with thoughts of touring the "Shaky Isles" on his Norton Dominator.

On his return from the Club he returned to the laptop to investigate similar tours of Great Britain. He quickly found that the unfavourable exchange rate made holidays in the UK and Europe about double what they were across the Tasman. The old mechanic was in two minds when he eventually went to bed: should he splurge on a trip to the "Old Country" or make the sensible choice and ride New Zealand.

An abundance of classic motorcycles greeted the three mechanics the following morning, so it was fortuitous that the old mechanic's restoration of the Velocette had stalled once more, awaiting the completion of the painting of the fuel tank. He would not get the tank returned until the end of the following week. After giving the front mudguard a light sand, he gave it another coat of undercoat and left it to dry.

As the three men gathered around the boiling jug, Michael asked, 'Have you thought any further about your holiday?'

'Yeah, I had a look at the magazine article again last night, and then compared it to holidays in Great Britain.'

'What did you decide?'

'I decided not to make a decision ... well, at least not now. With Katie due at the end of August, you'll prob'ly be wantin' some time off, and then spring's our busiest time, so we'll need all hands on deck. If the New Zealand trip's a success, they'll prob'ly have others planned in the followin' years.'

'And if its not?'

'Then I won't have wasted me money.'

'I don't know why ya wanna go overseas to ride ya bike,' contended Kieran, 'when there're plen'y o' good roads at 'ome.'

'I've already ridden most of the best ones,' countered the old mechanic. 'But you're right, there *are* plenty of good rides here.'

''Ave ya been down the Great Ocean Road an' over the Snowy Moun'ains 'Ighway?'

'Yep, and Bells, and the Back Spur, the Putty and the Oxley.'

'Where 'aven't ya been?'

'You know the song, "I've Been Everywhere Man".'

'I'm plannin' on goin' for a ride Sund'y arvo, ya wanna come Mike?' enquired Kieran.

'I thought you had church on Sundays,' queried Michael.

'We 'ave it in the mornin', but Lilly 'as ta go to 'er auntie's for a birthd'y celebration in the afternoon, so I'm free.'

'I thought you'd want to go and have sticky buns with your fiancés relatives?' teased the old mechanic.

'I don't even like me own relloes, so I'm not real keen on anyone else's, even Lilly's.'

'Um, well I'll need to check with Katie, but yeah, I'd love to go for a ride with you. Where do you plan on goin'?'

'I was thinkin' o' doin' the Oxley down to Gingers Creek an' back.'

'Well, don't forget, there're a lot of ratbags ride the Oxley on weekends,' cautioned the old mechanic, 'as well as the odd tourist towin' a caravan.'

'I 'ate caravans on windy roads,' remarked Kieran.

When the three mechanics broke for morning smoko, Michael called Katie at her office in Tamworth. When he had hung up he gave the thumbs-up signal to Kieran, 'Katie's got a baby shower to go to, so I'm free to go and do whatever I like.'

'Yay, party time!'

# Chapter 22

# A DEADLY SPIKE

The old mechanic had never ridden with Kieran, and it had been quite some time since he had been out on a motorcycle with Michael, so he decided he would join the other two on their Sunday ride. But, just in case he needed to make a last-minute change of plans, he did not give them advance notice; he would just turn up on the day.

The two younger mechanics planned to leave from Michael's unit at midday. The journey from Banjo Creek to the Ginger's Creek Roadhouse and return is around four hours via the highway, or six hours if you take the most direct route. While it may seem counter-intuitive that the more direct route is slower, the reason is that higher average speeds are able to be maintained on the highway. However, the highway is boring and heavily policed, so the pair decided to take the shorter route.

Michael and Kieran were just about to leave when the old mechanic arrived on his Norton Dominator.

'What are you doing here?' asked Michael. 'Katie's not here, she's already left.'

'I'm not here to see Katie,' informed the old mechanic, 'I wanna come for a ride with you guys.'

'Are ya worried you're gonna miss out on all the fun?' asked Kieran.

'Exactly!'

'Do you think you'll be able to keep up?' queried Michael with a cheeky grin.

'Don't you worry about me; if anything, it'll be me having to slow down for you pair. They didn't call my bike "The Dominator" for nothin', you know.'

'It's not the bike that's the problem,' suggested Kieran.

'Yeah, yeah, yeah. You jus' wait 'n see who's laughin' when we get to Ginger's Creek.'

When the three riders departed Banjo Creek, they rode relatively sedately, but once they had left the built-up area, the pace started to heat up. While two of the three bikes were the sportbikes of their eras, with their larger diameter wheels and narrow tyres, they would not be able to compete with more modern machinery. Nevertheless, the three riders rode their motorcycles to near the limits of their bike's capabilities, if not their own.

With one machine being a single and the other two twins, they all had quite narrow profiles, especially when compared to Japanese four-cylinder motorbikes, and so the available lean angle was comparatively greater before something touched down. The limiting factor then, was not the footpegs or the centre-stand scraping, but the available grip of the tyres, which tended to slide at the limits of adhesion. The upshot was that the trio could have more fun at slower speeds than riders of more modern machines.

The back road to Walcha was narrow and very windy. The three riders relished the challenge of keeping a good pace without doing anything stupid. Michael had the easiest ride as the large pulses of his big single cylinder engine meant that he could leave the bike in third or fourth gear and let the torque propel him from corner to corner. He only used the overdrive fifth gear on the longer stretches of road.

The old mechanic was enjoying himself, even though he was having to ride harder than he normally would to keep up. As so often happens when three motorcyclists ride together for the first time, competitive juices begin to flow as each one tries to outdo the other two. When his front tyre lost traction for the third time, he decided to slow down reasoning that it was better to come last than to "come a cropper".

Michael, who was in front of the old mechanic but behind Kieran, tried his hardest to stay with the Triumph Bonneville, but Kieran ultimately left him in his wake. Michael eventually slowed to let his father-in-law catch up so they could ride together. The two Norton riders would not see Kieran again until they entered the small township of Walcha.

'What took ya so long?' asked Kieran, when the other two riders parked their machines beside his bike.

'Common sense!' replied the old mechanic.

'I thought we were supposed to be riding together,' argued Michael. 'It wasn't supposed to be a race.'

'I'm with Mike there,' added the old mechanic.

'I wasn't racin',' countered Kieran, 'I was jus' ridin' at a good pace.'

'Yeah, a *race* pace. Why don't you let me set the pace and you follow me?'

'Sounds like a good idea to me,' enthused Michael.

'Yeah alright, but don't hold us up when we come to the best bits.'

After refuelling, the three set off for Ginger's Creek.

About a half hour's drive east of Walcha is the small community of Yarrowitch. It was not really a village, having little much more than a schoolhouse and a community hall, supported by a number of surrounding hobby farms, as well as a couple of sheep properties. There were no shops, or anywhere to buy supplies. If you needed food or fuel, you had to drive back to Walcha or further on to the "big smoke" of

Armidale or Tamworth. There were no telephones or mobile phone reception.

Bryan Timmons and his wife Faye had recently purchased a small allotment of about three hectares just off the Oxley Highway that they planned to turn into their "own little piece of paradise"; it was their idea of a "tree change". Bryan was busy that Sunday morning clearing much of the rubbish that still littered the block: rolls of barbed wire, old pieces of corrugated iron sheeting, bits of old star pickets and "reo", and small blocks of concrete, most of it rusted and good for nothing but the dump.

The local council rubbish tip was just outside Walcha. While it would have been easier for Bryan to dump the rubbish in the bush, as a conservationist, he abhorred the practice. After loading up his old flat-bed Holden one-ton utility with all the rubbish it would hold, he placed sheets of corrugated iron over the top as a covering, before tying it off with a couple of old pieces of rope. He turned onto the highway heading west just after the three motorcycles passed by heading in the opposite direction. But as he turned onto the highway, an unsecured rusty steel spike slid off the side of his truck and onto the roadway, unnoticed. It would remain there unnoticed for hours.

The first section of the Oxley Highway passes through farm land and is relatively straight, wide and smooth. But the road narrows as it enters the state forest and becomes tight and twisty. Indeed, it boasts an advisory road sign that reads "Winding Road Next 45 Km". No wonder then that it draws motorcyclists like moths to a candle.

The three riders were enjoying the good pace that the old mechanic was setting for them. In some sections, Kieran wished that he would go faster, and in others Michael had trouble keeping up, but overall, the ride was both pleasurable and challenging. For the old mechanic, he loved the feel of the road brushing the outsides of his leather boots as he swung from side to side and corner to corner. The strong eucalyptus smell of the Australian bush made him feel fresh and invigorated. Riding the bike of his dreams with his mates on one of the best roads in the country; could life get any better he wondered.

All too soon they arrived at the Ginger's Creek Roadhouse. While fuel was available, none of the trio needed much more than a toilet break and a cold drink.

'How good was 'at road?' asked Kieran rhetorically. 'I don't think I've ever seen so many corners in such a short distance. I don't think ridin' 'round Philip Island a hundred times'd be any better.'

'I'd get bored goin' around the same track more than a couple of times,' suggested Michael. 'This road is the duck's guts.'

'How was the pace,' asked the old mechanic, 'too fast, too slow, or just right?'

'It was fine for me,' answered Michael.

'Yeah, it was okay,' Kieran replied. 'I found I could relax a bit an' enjoy the scenery.'

'What scenery? There was nothin' but trees,' insisted the old mechanic.

'And big ones at that,' responded Kieran with a grin.

They all burst into laughter.

'Who wants to lead goin' back?' invited the old mechanic.

'My turn!' replied Michael without hesitation.

'Just be careful on some of them corners, Mike, they can tighten up on you. Sometimes it's best to trail-brake comin' into the bend and then accelerate out.'

'Yeah, will do.'

The return ride was that much more relaxed as Michael set the pace. While he was enjoying powering out of the corners and using engine braking to slow his Norton for the next bend, the pace was frustrating Kieran. So much so that when the road opened out, he overtook Michael's bike and accelerated away.

After giving his Bonneville its head, he slowed again and pulled over to wait for the others to catch up. As Michael went past, he pulled back onto the road and followed in behind, with the old mechanic playing "tail-end Charlie".

At about the same time that the three riders left Ginger's Creek, a mid-sized truck left Walcha loaded with sheep, heading for the sale yards at Wauchope. Michael passed the truck just before the intersection with Carey's Road. The truck driver drove over the steel spike that had earlier fallen from Bryan Timmons' truck. The spike was flung up into the air and struck, point first, the visor of Kieran's helmet. It penetrated the visor and pierced his skull just above his left eye.

Kieran blacked out immediately. His bike left the road at more or less the 100 kmh speed limit and hit the embankment before crashing heavily. The rider was flung from his bike and lay motionless in a shallow ditch beside the road. The truck driver did not see what happened, and he did not stop.

The old mechanic braked heavily when he saw Kieran's motorcycle run off the road and crash. He parked his bike on the verge and ran back to attend to Kieran. Michael did not notice that the others had stopped until he checked his rear-view mirror about half a kilometre up the road. He stopped for a brief moment before turning around to see what was holding up the others. Michael arrived to find the old mechanic bent over Kieran who was prone by the roadside.

'Mike, quick, call for an ambulance,' ordered the old mechanic, 'and the police.'

Michael dug in his pockets for his phone. He checked for reception, but there was none. 'I haven't got any reception. I need to get closer in to Walcha.'

'Okay, but hurry.'

Kieran's breathing was very shallow. The old mechanic tried to make him comfortable, but he was unable to remove the younger man's helmet because of the spike sticking out. He was able to remove the screws holding the visor which allowed him fresh air. A few people in cars stopped to offer assistance, and one even gave them a blanket to keep the patient warm.

The ambulance and police from Walcha arrived together, nearly half an hour after the accident. While there was a hospital at Walcha, it was ill equipped to deal with such traumatic injuries as incurred by Kieran. The ambulance crew called in the rescue helicopter to transport the patient to the John Hunter Hospital in Newcastle. It landed in the corner of the field owned by Bryan Timmons. Kieran suffered cardiac arrest enroute.

The old mechanic threw up after the ambulance left. The police senior constable took a brief statement on the roadside, before arranging for a tow-truck to pick up Kieran's crashed Triumph Bonneville.

The two men rode home at a more sedate pace, each lost in his own thoughts. They did not arrive home until after 8:00 pm. Michael had called Katie in Walcha to say he had been delayed, but he did not tell her the full extent of Kieran's injuries until after he arrived home.

The police had already telephoned through to their counterparts in Tamworth to notify Kieran's next-of-kin. John Traeghier and his wife drove straight to Lilly's place to inform her of the accident before heading to Newcastle. Lilly was distraught.

# Chapter 23

# IMPOSSIBLE CHOICES

Kieran was revived in the helicopter as he was being air-lifted to the John Hunter Hospital. The mobile Intensive Care Team made the difficult decision to remove the rider's badly damaged helmet without moving the spike embedded in his forehead. They believed it was a case of lose the helmet or else lose the patient.

The rescue helicopter arrived at the hospital helipad in Newcastle with Kieran barely clinging to life. The emergency staff rushed him straight into the operating theatre. The spike, as well as a large part of his skull, was removed to relieve the pressure on his brain. The neurosurgical team worked on him for six hours to stabilise him. He was placed on life support in an induced coma.

His parents arrived with Kieran still in theatre. When the surgical team had done all they could to save their son's life, the senior neurosurgeon met them in the waiting room; it was after 1:00 am.

''Ow is 'e doc?' asked John Traeghier.

'Not good, I'm afraid. I won't beat around the bush; after the trauma he's suffered, it's a miracle he's survived to this point.'

On hearing the news, Mrs Traeghier broke down weeping.

'Can we see 'im?'

'He's in a coma in intensive care. He won't be able to hear you.'

'That's alright, we jus' wanna see 'im.'

Michael and Katie arrived late for work the following morning. There had been no news about Kieran. Katie had tried to call Lilly's mobile, but it went straight through to voicemail. Lilly had actually taken leave from her job and had driven straight to Newcastle in the early hours of Monday morning to be by her man. She would stay with relatives at New Lambton, just five minutes from the hospital.

The old mechanic opened up the workshop just after 7:00 am and had been dealing with their customers. He had thought about not opening the doors at all that morning but several bikes had already been booked in for work to be done; he could not disappoint their regulars.

Everyone was in a sombre mood when they came together over a cuppa.

'What exactly happened?' asked Katie of her father.

'I was about twenty bike lengths behind Kieran when a truck went past. I think something must've either fallen off the truck or was flung up by the tyres and hit Kieran through his visor. Next thing I know he's run off the road and crashed.'

'Did the truck driver stop?'

'No, he probably didn't even see what happened.'

'You know it could've been any one of us,' pondered Michael. 'Kieran just happened to be in the wrong place at the wrong time. Ten seconds either way and nobody would've been hit.'

'Or five seconds either way and it could've been you, or it could've been me,' suggested the old mechanic.

Thank God it was not either of you, thought Katie selfishly.

'Do you think he'll pull through?' asked Michael.

'I don't know Mike. That steel spike went right into his skull. I don't know how deep it penetrated, but ... It's got to have done a lot of damage.'

Later in the morning when Katie rang the hospital for information, she was told he was in a "critical condition in intensive care".

Lilly arrived at the John Hunter Hospital mid-morning and went straight to Reception to enquire after Kieran. She was merely given the routine response that he was in a "critical condition in intensive care". But when she asked if she could see him, permission was denied as she was not listed as his "immediate family".

'But I'm his fiancé,' pleaded Lilly.

'I'm sorry dear,' replied the receptionist, 'it's only *immediate* family.'

'But we're getting married in October.'

'I'm sorry, but I do have my orders.'

Lilly looked around anxiously. There were signs everywhere, but none of them pointed to the Intensive Care Unit. Finally admitting defeat, she said a short prayer before heading to the cafeteria where she would decide on a course of action. Even though she had skipped breakfast, she did not feel all that hungry, though the smell of coffee was enticing. It seemed her prayer was answered though, because in a corner, she saw Mrs Traeghier having a pot of tea.

She rushed over to her table, 'Hello Mrs Traeghier, how's Kieran?'

Mrs Traeghier was startled, having been lost in thought. 'Hello Lilly dear. He's ...' Tears started to well in her eyes. She dabbed at them with a tissue before blowing her nose. 'He's not very good I'm afraid.' She started crying again as she remembered seeing her son and youngest child with the top of his head bandaged and tubes protruding from his mouth and nose.

'They won't let me see him,' lamented Lilly.

Despite her sorrow, Mrs Traeghier was outraged. 'Come with me dear, I'll take you to him.'

As they stepped into the lift, Lilly asked, 'Where's Mr Traeghier?'

'He's keeping vigil dear; he doesn't want to leave Kieran's bedside, just in case he wakes up.'

'Do you think he'll wake up soon?'

Mrs Traeghier did not answer. On the third floor, the pair emerged from the lift, turning left into the corridor. At the end, they approached a glass panelled door with a telephone hanging from the wall. Mrs Traeghier picked up the telephone and spoke briefly to the nurse who answered.

'They only allow two visitors at a time Lilly dear. You go in; the nurse'll show you where he is. I'll be in the cafeteria downstairs.'

'Thanks Mrs Traeghier.'

Lilly kissed and hugged her future mother-in-law, as the nurse in charge opened the door to allow her inside the Intensive Care Unit. She followed the nurse through the ICU to the room where Kieran was located. She was shocked to see him hooked up to so many machines, monitors and intravenous drips. He was almost unrecognisable. Mr Traeghier was sitting in a chair by his bedside. When he recognised her, he rose from the chair and hugged her. She sobbed in his shoulder.

In difficult circumstances, the old mechanic always found solace in his work. He could usually forget all about his own troubles and difficulties by getting back to business. Even when his wife was in hospital with breast cancer, he had immersed himself servicing and repairing his customer's classic motorcycles. Indeed, if he had not done so, his business likely would have gone under. The only time he could remember that he could not work was when Katie had been in hospital after the accident that claimed her then partner, Kevin. Michael was his saving grace on that occasion.

After giving the front mudguard of the Velocette Venom its first coat of black gloss enamel, the old mechanic joined Michael in working on a variety of classic British motorcycles. Katie busied herself with the administration of the business: invoicing, stock management and preparing the Business Activity Statements for the GST. They broke, as was their custom, for smoko, but the usual light banter was missing.

When everyone was sipping their mugs of tea, Katie remarked, 'I really feel sorry for Lilly.'

'Why's that?' asked Michael.

'She was so looking forward to the wedding. She'd already picked out her dress. You know she asked me to be her Matron-of-Honour.'

'It's still five months away. Kieran should be up and about by then.'

'I'd like to think so, but I'd be surprised,' mused the old mechanic. 'This whole thing's turned the lives of everyone upside down. I reckon if Kieran survives the week, it'll be a miracle.'

The week dragged on. There had been no improvement in Kieran's condition; he remained in a coma on life support in intensive care. Lilly and the Traeghiers had been playing tag team, one keeping watch on the patient, while one ate and another slept.

Kieran's two sisters had been and gone; so too Lilly's parents. Katie finally got through to Lilly by phone, but there was little she could say amidst the tears on both ends of the phone. But the message was clear: Kieran was in a bad way.

Five days after the accident, the team of neurosurgeons ran a series of tests on Kieran to gauge the extent of brain damage that had been incurred. When the testing had been concluded, the senior neurosurgeon met with the Traeghiers and Lilly.

'As you know, Kieran incurred significant trauma to his left frontal lobe. The damage was so extensive that we had to remove the top part of his skull from just above his left eye. The metal spike penetrated roughly eight centimetres into his brain. There was a lot of bleeding and a lot of damage. This morning we ran a series of tests on Kieran's brain functions. From that, we've concluded that he has no chance of surviving if he's removed from life support.'

'What're you sayin' doc; that he's brain dead?' queried John Traeghier who was shocked at the pronouncement.

'To put it bluntly, yes.'

Both women burst into tears.

'Isn't there anythin' more you c'n do?'

'We've done everything possible. If there was any hope that he could recover, I'd tell you. But I think it's only fair that I tell you that there is no hope.'

'When're you gonna turn off 'is life support? Can we see 'im first?'

'We're not going to turn it off right away. But I do need to ask you if you're willing to consent to donating his organs.'

John and his wife had already discussed with their children that they would want to donate their organs in the event of their untimely death. But they had not reckoned on being asked to donate their children's organs. Kieran and Lilly had not discussed the subject, even though both had indicated their willingness to do so on their driver's licence. In the end, all three found it confronting to have to decide for someone who was the object of their deepest love and affection.

With tears in his eyes John asked, 'When d'ya need ta know?'

'We'd like to know as soon as possible so we can organise those on the organ waiting list to be prepared and admitted.'

'But you're not gonna pull the plug straight away, are ya?'

'No, of course not; we won't do anything 'til Monday now.'

'When can we take 'im 'ome?'

'Probably Tuesday or Wednesday.'

The old mechanic had given the front mudguard a couple more coats of enamel paint. On the Friday he had collected the fuel tank from his painter, and on the Monday morning he started putting the Velocette Venom Clubman back together.

Monday morning was also the time that Kieran's life support was turned off. His heart, liver and kidneys saved the lives of four people, and his corneas saved the sight of another two. But it was cold comfort to the Lilly and Traeghiers.

The news of Kieran's passing hit the two mechanics particularly hard. Not only was the youngest motorcycle mechanic an excellent tradesman, but he was also a close colleague and a good friend, and for Michael, Kieran had become his best mate – his "cobber".

The funeral service, held the following week, was held in the chapel of the funeral home. It was full to overflowing. Following a short service, a procession of classic motorcycles, made up of friends and clients, led the funeral cortege to the cemetery where the senior pastor of Kieran's church interred his mortal remains.

The wake was held in the function room of the South Tamworth Bowling Club. None of his church friends attended, except Lilly and her parents.

Lilly's emotions were numb. She had cried a river of tears over the preceding fortnight. Everything she had ever dreamed of, all the plans she had made; her hopes and her joys had all died, along with her fiancé. Kieran was the best thing that had ever happened to her, and now he was gone.

# Chapter 24

# AN UNEXPECTED DELIVERY

The old mechanic had completed the restoration of the 1966 Velocette Venom Clubman Mark2. He had offered the motorcycle for sale on eBay, but bidding was slow, and it did not reach its reserve price before the auction concluded. The bike was also listed on Gumtree but, other than a couple of "scammers", the machine had not attracted any serious attention.

Kieran's Triumph Bonneville had been retrieved from Walcha. John Traeghier had indicated that his wife did not wish to have it at their home, so he asked the old mechanic if he would store the machine while they decided what to do with it. The motorcycle itself was not badly damaged, unlike the man who last rode it.

Michael had changed their working routine out of necessity. Now with only two mechanics, the motorcycle restorations would need to take a "back-seat" to the core business of servicing and repairing the classic bikes of their customers. Only when their main concern was quiet would the restorations resume. Even though winter had started, the normal slowdown associated with the colder months had not yet commenced. Indeed, if anything, the workshop was busier than normal.

The two mechanics and Katie came together for morning smoko. Katie had started to waddle as the baby in her bulging belly grew.

'How many months are you now sweetheart?' asked the old mechanic.

'I'm supposed to be 28 weeks, but I think we might've miscalculated.'

'Why do you say that?' asked Michael.

'Well, I think I started counting from when my period was due, and not from the date of conception.'

'Do you mean to say you're more pregnant than you thought you were?'

Katie and the old mechanic laughed at the statement.

'No silly, I can't be any more pregnant than I am now. But the baby might be coming earlier than we've been planning; that's what the obstetrician reckons anyhow.'

'How much earlier?'

'Two weeks, maybe more.'

'Have you thought of names for it yet?' enquired the old mechanic.

'We've got a list of names for both boys and girls, but we haven't chosen any yet. I like …'

Before she could finish the sentence, the telephone started to ring. She picked up the phone mid-sentence.

'Hello, Classic Bike Repairs and Service, Katie speaking.'

'*Um, hello, um, does someone by the name of George Edwards work there?*'

'Yes, just a moment please; I'll get him for you.'

Katie motioned for her father to come and answer the phone.

'Hello, George Edwards; how can I help you?'

'*Um, hello Mr Edwards, um, I was talking with an old friend of mine, and, um, he told me he sold his classic motorcycle to you, a Velocette Venom Clubman, and um, that you planned to restore it and, um, I was wondering if you've finished it yet?*'

'As a matter of fact, I've not only finished the restoration, but it's currently for sale.'

'*Oh, please don't sell it, Mr Edwards; I want it.*'

'What's your name?'

'*Um, Stanley ... Stanley Baxter.*'

'Hello Stanley, please call me George.'

'*Thank you George.*'

'Do you live in Sydney too, Stanley?'

'*Oh, no, I live in Mudgee. Um, how much were you asking for the bike?*'

'I'd been expecting it to go for around the $25,000 mark on eBay. But it didn't even reach my reserve price. Did you have a figure in mind?'

'*I'd want to have a look at the bike first before I made you an offer. Would you be happy to hold it for me until I could arrange to come and see it?*'

'Well, without a holding deposit, I'd only be willing to keep it until the weekend. If you haven't come up here to see it by close of business Friday, I'll be putting it back on the market. But if I get a firm offer in the mean time, I'll be selling it. Okay?'

'*Okay George, that's a fair deal. But if you do get a firm offer, would you please let me know?*'

'Sure Stanley, give me your number.'

The old mechanic did not receive any other substantial offers. Stanley arrived at the workshop with his son mid-morning Friday. After eye-balling the Velocette, they made an offer of $22,500, which the old mechanic accepted. It turned out that Stanley and Kelvin were old school mates and that there was a degree of rivalry between the two, which had carried over to the next generation. What one wanted, the other had to have. But where Kelvin had the wherewithal to restore the

Velocette, Stanley instead had the money to pay someone else to do it for him. The old mechanic just hoped that the son would not follow his friend by falling off his newly restored motorbike.

After the old mechanic had farewelled the father and son duo, the thought struck him that the lives of two much loved sons had been changed forever due to head injuries incurred in a motorcycle accident that was not the fault of either rider. And both had been riding newly restored machines. Over lunch, he shared his thoughts with Michael.

'It just doesn't seem fair,' mused Michael, 'two people, minding their own business, riding within the road rules … one dies and the other has brain damage for the rest of his life.'

'Yep, life does seem unfair at times.'

'I'm not sure which'd be worse.'

'What?'

'Dying or suffering brain damage for the rest of your life.'

'I suppose it depends on how severe the damage is, and where you're at in life.'

'I suppose Kieran's better off dead than living as a vegetable.'

'From speaking with John Traeghier, Kieran was as good as dead the moment that piece of steel struck him. It was only the machines that were keeping him alive.'

'I miss him, George,' admitted Michael, a tear forming in the corner of his eye.

'I think we all do, Mike.'

Michael wiped the tear away and blew his nose.

'Changing the subject,' he continued, 'how much did we make on the Velocette?'

'About twelve grand all up, I think.'

'So that's about $30,000 from the two bikes, so far. I didn't think it'd be so lucrative when I first suggested you do this for a living.'

'Yeah, you might be able to start payin' me one o' these days.'

'Yeah, I suppose that's only fair too. And we should be able to afford you now that we have one less on the payroll.'

'Does that mean I'll be able to save up for that holiday to the UK?'

'Maybe! But it'll mean you'll no longer be an Emeritus Mechanic.'

'I can live with that.'

Michael arrived home to the smell of cooking. He followed his nose into the kitchen where he found Katie preparing vegetables.

'Hmm, something smells good my darling. What's on the me-n-u for dinner tonight?' he asked as he embraced his wife from behind.

'Hello Mikey. Slow-cooked pork belly with all the trimmings – if you've been a good boy today.'

'Today? I'm a good boy every day.'

'Well, you'd better hurry up and have a shower; dinner'll be ready soon.'

Michael started shedding his work clothes as he headed toward their bedroom. When he had turned on the shower he called from the bathroom, 'George sold the Velocette this morning.'

'That's good. How much did we get for it?'

'I'm not sure, but he said we'd made a profit of around twelve grand.'

'That's good.'

Michael returned to the kitchen just as Katie was removing the roasting pan from the oven.

'Would you set the table please?' she asked.

'Of course; are we having dessert?'

'Yeah, if you want it, and you can fit it in.' Katie smiled.

'I'll wait 'n see.'

'Would you sharpen the carving knife?'

'Okay! Do you want me to carve it too?'

'Yes please, but don't give me too much.'

The pork belly had a thick layer of crackling which crunched as Michael pressed the carving knife into it.

'I don't know what I prefer more: the taste of crackling or the sound,' remarked Michael.

'I think the sound enhances the taste,' suggested Katie.

'Yeah, probably.'

The pair thoroughly enjoyed their meal. Michael even had dessert, while Katie passed, suggesting that with a "belly full of arms and legs", there was no room for anything more. In return for the deliciously cooked dinner, Michael cleared the table and stacked the dishwasher. Katie was given time out to put her feet up and watch some television.

As she sat on the lounge chair, Katie felt uncomfortable, as if she had eaten too much. She felt a pain in her stomach like a bad case of indigestion.

'Mikey, would you get me some of those tablets to ease indigestion please?' she asked.

'Why, did you eat too much?' he teased.

'No, I didn't have any more than I usually have.'

'They're not labour pains, are they?'

'Of course not; the baby's not due for at least another two months … I think,' Katie replied out loud, but to herself she added, I hope.

The pain in her stomach abated somewhat, so she went to bed. But later that night, it returned. She got up, being careful not to wake Michael, and went for a walk around the unit. But the pain continued into the early hours of the morning. Eventually, Katie had to wake her husband.

'Mikey! Mikey! Wake up; I think the baby's coming.'

Michael became instantly awake. Katie threw some personal items into an overnight bag while Michael quickly dressed. He retrieved the car from the garage while she locked the front door to their unit.

'I thought you said it wasn't due for another two months,' Michael stated when they had pulled out onto the New England Highway for the drive into Tamworth.

'The baby's not due, but it obviously has its own timetable.'

Michael drove at more or less the speed limit. There was little traffic; the Friday night revellers seeming to have gone to bed early. And though he was pretty sure that the police had most likely already gone back to the station for the night, he did not want to have to explain why he was speeding. He pulled up outside the Emergency Department and ran inside to get assistance for his wife. An orderly wheeled out a wheelchair for the patient.

After moving his car to the hospital's visitor parking lot, Michael returned to find that his wife had been transferred to the maternity unit. He found her with an IV drip in her right arm and a blood pressure monitor on her left.

'How're you feeling?' he asked.

'Alright, I think.'

'Where is everybody? I thought you'd have someone lookin' after you.'

'They're busy. The told me to buzz them if the contractions came closer than one every five minutes.'

'What's the drip for?'

'Pain relief, and to try to slow the contractions down.'

Michael sat on the chair provided and Katie started to doze. A nurse came into the room to check on her progress.

'How are you feeling?' she asked.

'Okay, I think.'

'How far apart are the contractions?'

Katie looked at her watch, 'About ten minutes.'

Another contraction came causing Katie to wince in pain. When her water broke, she was moved into the birthing room, and the Neonatal Intensive Care Unit was put on standby. Michael was given a gown, cap and mask to wear so that he could be a part of the process.

Katie gave birth to a baby boy six weeks premature at 7:17 am, weighing just 2.1 kilograms and 45 centimetres long. He was immediately placed in a humidicrib. The mother returned to the maternity ward exhausted.

Michael was elated over the birth of his son. As soon as he had taken some photos of his baby boy, he posted them to Facebook, before calling his mother to give her the good news. Just before 8:30 am he called the old mechanic.

'*Hello.*'

'Hello George, it's Michael.'

'*Hello Mike, is everything okay?*'

'Yes, Grandad. Katie gave birth this morning.'

'*This morning? Is she alright?*'

'Yes, she's fine.'

'*And the baby?*'

'A little boy. He'll be alright. He's in a humidicrib in Intensive Care, but they said he'll be just fine.'

'*Do you have a name yet?*'

'Yeah, Kieran George Jones.'

# Chapter 25

# THE IMPORTANT THINGS IN LIFE

The old mechanic had been into the hospital on both Saturday and Sunday to see his daughter and brand-new baby grandson. Baby Kieran was small; indeed, he had never seen an infant so tiny in his life. He was slightly jaundiced, but otherwise healthy. Katie looked radiant, and after a well-earned rest on Saturday morning, she was up and about. She had been able to express milk to feed her baby while he was in the humidicrib. She was hopeful that she would soon be able to breast-feed him. Michael was very pleased with himself, and told anyone who would listen about the baby.

On the following Monday morning the old mechanic woke early. He had not slept well and had a stiff neck with pins and needles down his left arm that he put down to lying poorly in bed. He washed his face and shaved before preparing his usual breakfast of tea and toast. He was not sure if Michael would be coming in to work, so he expected that he would be very busy.

At about 6:30 am he opened the workshop. As it turned out, while a large number of customers called in at the workshop, the majority did so simply to congratulate the old mechanic on the news of the birth of his first grandchild, and to pass on their best wishes to the new mum and dad.

With only a half dozen motorcycles to work on, he started, as usual, with a cuppa. As he surveyed the workshop, he thought about the comings and goings of the past five years. Hundreds, if not thousands of classic motorcycles had been serviced, repaired and otherwise maintained, four classics had been restored, returning them to useable service, and many more had been modified to make them even more useable.

Then he thought about all the people who had come and gone. Some had moved away, while others had arrived into the area. Too many had passed away. Again, he thought of Kieran. His Triumph Bonneville was still parked in the workshop, albeit concealed under a tarpaulin, both to protect it and to keep it from view. But its presence was a constant reminder of the man and the accident that claimed his life.

His thoughts eventually drifted to his new baby grandson. He wondered whether he would follow in his father's, grandfather's and great-grandfather's footsteps in becoming a motorcycle mechanic, or whether he would try his hand at something else. While classic British motorcycles had grown in popularity in the past five years, he began to wonder if the trend would continue. Fashions come and go; what was once popular is now old hat. He smiled at the thought: classic British motorcycles are popular simply because they are old fashioned.

'Well,' the old mechanic said to himself, 'nothing's gonna get done sittin' on ya duff.'

In the workshop that morning was a Triumph Trident triple that needed a tune up as it was running roughly, a Triumph TR6 Trophy and a BSA A10 Lightning needing a service, a Matchless G80CSR needing new brake shoes, a Royal Enfield Bullet needing new points and a Norton ES2 needing the clutch adjusted.

The old mechanic was a firm believer in getting the easiest and simplest jobs done first; leaving the more difficult and time-consuming ones until last. That meant he would start with the Norton and finish with the Trident.

The stiffness in his neck had not lessened as the morning progressed. Indeed, if anything, by smoko time, it seemed to have travelled to his left shoulder. As the jug boiled for his cuppa, he rummaged through the drawers of Katie's desk looking for some paracetamol. It was there that he collapsed with an excruciating pain in his chest.

Michael did arrive for work, but later than usual. He had initially expected that Katie would be coming home that morning, leaving her baby in the hospital. However, a change of heart by the nursing staff meant that she would remain in hospital for at least another day.

Riding his Norton, Michael manoeuvred his way down the laneway outside the workshop. After parking his motorcycle, and taking off his helmet, jacket and gloves, he was surprised at how quiet the morning was.

'Hello,' he called as he entered the workshop, 'is anybody here?'

There was no reply but the chirping of sparrows outside.

Michael's initial thought was that the old mechanic had gone for a toilet break, but as the minutes passed, he became concerned. Eventually, he found his father-in-law sprawled on the floor in Katie's office.

The old mechanic was unconscious. Michael checked for a pulse – it was faint, and his breathing was shallow. He dialled 000 on the telephone in Katie's office.

*'Hello, what is your emergency?'*

Michael gave the details of what he thought had occurred to the operator, and where he was located. The ambulance paramedic arrived about 12 minutes after the call. They loaded the patient on board and left with lights flashing and sirens wailing.

The younger mechanic was in two minds about what to do. Katie needed to know that her father had been taken to hospital with a suspected heart attack. However, he wanted to be with her when she was told. But he also had an obligation to their customers. In the end, he decided to tell her by phone.

'Hello Katie, it's Mike.'

*'Hello Mikey, what's up? Do ya miss me already?'*

'Um, I arrived at the workshop and found George on the floor in your office. The paramedic thinks he's had a heart attack.'

There was silence on the end of the phone.

'Are you still there?'

Now in tears she replied, *'Yes. Where is he now?'*

'They've taken him to the hospital, so I expect he'd be there by now.'

*'What are you going to do?'*

'There's still work to be done here. He must've been half way through the various jobs. I'll need to see where he was up to and continue fixing the bikes. Then I'll hafta stay 'til the different customers pick them up.'

*'Mikey.'*

'Yes.'

*'I don't want to lose him too.'*

'I'm sure he'll be fine my darling,' Michael consoled his wife. 'He's in the best of care.'

The ambulance arrived at the Tamworth Base Hospital Accident and Emergency Department with the old mechanic barely clinging to life. The paramedic needed to revive him enroute as his heart had stopped beating and he had stopped breathing.

Katie asked the sister in charge of the maternity ward to contact A&E to find out what was happening to her father. The news was that he had been taken in to surgery for an emergency by-pass operation. Even though he had quit cigarettes in recent years, the accumulation of many years of smoking and a diet high in cholesterol had taken its toll on his cardio-vascular system.

Later that evening, Michael found Katie in her room breast feeding Kieran. Her eyes were puffy and her nose red; she had clearly been crying recently.

'Are you alright?' he asked.

'Yeah, I'm okay, which is more than I can say about dad.'

'They told me he's in intensive care in the coronary unit.'

'Apparently his heart's been so badly damaged, he'll probably never be able to work again.'

'I'm sure he'll be okay.' He laughed. 'Tryin' to stop your old man from workin' is like tryin' to stop the frost from formin' in the winter months. It just can't happen. Even if he has ta use a wheelchair, he'll still keep comin' to the workshop.'

Katie smiled at the thought. 'Yeah, [sniff] you're probably right.'

'Changin' the subject, the little tacker seems to like suckin' on your boob. Mind you, I can't blame him.'

'Mi-key, don't say it like that. He's just hungry.'

'Yeah, so am I.'

The old mechanic regained consciousness later that night and he was moved out of ICU the following morning. He needed another operation to fit stents to clear two other blockages in arteries leading to his heart, so he was to remain in the Coronary Unit for another three days before being transferred to the Rehabilitation Unit.

Katie was released from hospital the same morning that her father came out of ICU. Baby Kieran needed to remain behind in hospital to ensure he gained a little more weight and to give his organs a little more time to develop. It would be another two more weeks before he arrived home at the unit in Banjo Creek, about the same time his grandfather returned home.

Michael had been juggling his responsibilities in the workshop with his desire to be with his wife and son, and visiting his father-in-law. Now as the sole mechanic, their customers had to rely on him alone. And with Katie's absence, he had to do much of the workshop paperwork as well. At least he could take that work home.

While the old mechanic had been in hospital, Katie had managed time to clean his house and restock his pantry. The hospital social worker had arranged for the local Home and Community Care Office to visit the old mechanic to determine what services he would require to enable him to continue living at home. He had been provided with a "walker", which he hated, and to have a ramp installed in place of the steps to his back door; he could tolerate the ramp.

Despite being put through an exercise program while he was in the Rehabilitation Unit of the hospital, he had lost a lot of condition and quickly became tired; even showering and dressing was an effort. But the old mechanic was determined to get well enough to return to his first love: fixing classic motorcycles. On the following Monday morning, even before the ramp had been installed, he managed to drag his walker down from the back porch and toddle his way over to the workshop where Michael was working.

'Morning Mike,' he called.

'Morning George, I'm surprised to see you up and about,' said Michael.

'I didn't want you to be lonely. And besides, there's no better place I'd rather be.'

'Do ya want a cuppa?'

'I thought you'd have had one waitin' for me?'

'I thought you'd be stayin' at home with your feet up watchin' the tele.'

'I had a gutful of daytime television when I was in the hospital. I'd rather watch paint dry than seein' any more of that garbage.'

Michael laughed.

'How's the bub?'

'He's fine. It's Katie who's havin' a hard time gettin' used to the four hourly feeds.'

The old mechanic smiled. 'It'll be a while before he'll be sleepin' right through the night.'

'So how're you feelin' now? How's the ticker?' asked Michael.

'Yeah, alright. Mind you, I didn't think I'd make it out of the hospital. It was just as well you found me when you did. They told me they had to revive me in the ambulance when my heart stopped.'

'Yeah, Katie was pretty upset when I told her; especially bein' so soon after Kieran's accident.'

'They reckon bad things come in threes, but I hope they're wrong.'

'Me too. Well, I've gotta get back to work. What are you gonna be doin'?'

'I c'n do the paperwork if ya like?' suggested the old mechanic.

'Are you sure you c'n manage?'

'Y-e-a-h, I'll be fine.'

'That'd be great if ya could.'

The old mechanic made his way slowly to the storeroom. The stock sheets revealed that there had been no orders for parts in over a month so that was his first priority. He also found that the bookkeeping was two weeks behind, so that was next. By mid-morning he had caught up.

'Time for smoko Mike,' he called.

'Okay, won't be a sec.'

Michael joined his father-in-law for their smoko break. When they began sipping their mugs of tea, the old mechanic spoke. 'You know Mike, lyin' in that hospital bed, not knowin' if I'd be makin' it out alive, I began thinkin' about life and my own mortality. There was Kieran, with his whole life ahead of him, enjoyin' life to the full, taken in his prime. Then there's me with most of my life behind me, but I live to fight another day.'

'Yeah, you just never know when your time's gonna be up.'

'It made me think about what's really important in life, and I can tell you now, it's not motorbikes.'

'So what *is* important?' enquired Michael.

'People; people and relationships; families and friends. What you do in life isn't anywhere near as important as who you're doin' it with. You c'n be the best motorcycle mechanic in the world, but when you're gone, no-one'll care or take more than a moment's notice. The people who will take notice are those closest to you. Make sure you're never too busy for the people who love ya the most.'

THE END

Printed in Great Britain
by Amazon